A Wood-Carver's Christmas Tale

Contact Marcie at www.marciesextro.com

All Scripture quotations are from the King James Version Bible.

"Now Are Lit A Thousand Christmas Candles" lyrics written by Emmy Kohler, 1898

"Now It's Christmas Time Again" lyrics written by Mads Hansen

"The Wood-Carver's Christmas Tale" is a work of fiction. The story, all names, characters, and incidents portrayed in this production are fictitious. No identification with actual persons (living or deceased), places, buildings, and products is intended or should be inferred.

Cover Design by 100 Covers

Edited by JB Wilson

Copyedited by Janet Seegebarth

A Wood-Carver's Christmas Tale

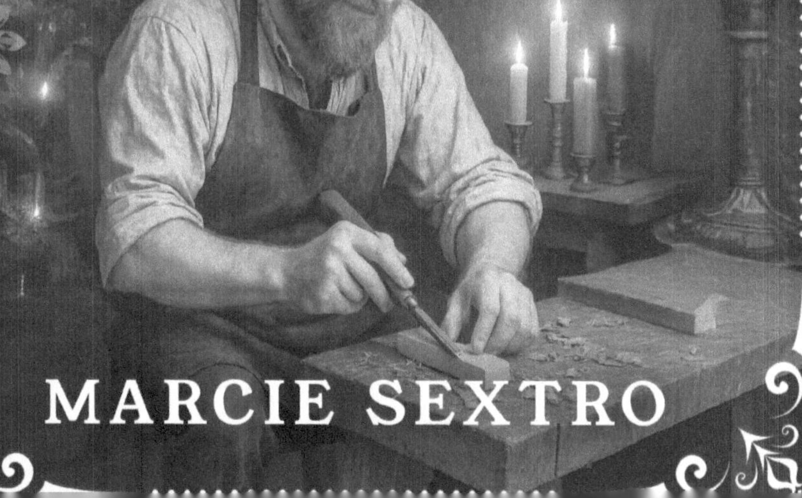

MARCIE SEXTRO

Dedication

To my loving Father and Co-Writer

Our time writing this book together

has been life altering.

I know You better, hear You better,

and love You now more than ever.

Characters

Wood-Carver Story Characters

- **Nils Kindberg**- Örebro's wood-carver, late 40s, kind and creative husband and father who has a strong relationship with the Creator (God)—the Creator guides him in what to carve and also gives him stories that go with each carving

- **Rachel Kindberg**- Nils's wife, late 40s, sees the needs of those hurting around her and has a heart for helping and ministering through the gifts the Creator has given her such as baking

- **Stefan Kindberg**- Nils and Rachel's son, 20s, gone for his 3-month conscription

- **Karl Vasa**- Duke of Örebro castle, late 40s, Elia's father, searching for help for his daughter

- **Sylvie Vasa**- Duchess of Örebro castle, Duke's wife, late 40s, Elia's mother

- **Elia Vasa**- Duke's daughter, ten years old, has been very ill

- **Countess Pernilla**- Duchess Sylvie's mother, Elia's grandmother

Castle Staff

- **Vincent**- manservant/butler of Örebro castle, 50s, married, extremely loyal and hardworking

- **Brigitta**- Vincent's wife, cook of Örebro castle, 50s, heart of gold

- **Alma**- Elia's nanny

- **Jesper**- footman

Townspeople

- **Klemens**- postman
- **Arne**- young boy
- **Charles Modine**- injured in a wagon accident, father
- **Fionda Modine**- Charles's wife, mother of four
- **Frederik Modine**- youngest son of Charles & Fionda
- **Ina Modine**- youngest daughter of Charles & Fionda
- **Jarl and Janna Modine**- twins of Charles and Fionda, oldest children, ten years old

Woodsman Story Characters

- **Anders Dahl**- woodsman, cabin/land in the woods by Söderhamn, married to Maja, 40s, orphan
- **Maja Dahl**- kindly wife of Anders, cheese maker, 40s
- **Ackermans**- Anders and Maja's neighbors

- **Leena Solberg**- orphan girl, ten years old, red hair
- **Hunched-back man**- cook at the fishing village
- **Rolf Solberg**- Leena's uncle, boss of the fishing village, hard man with no care for children

Anders & Maja's Farm Animals

- **Pip**- young, grey-capped chickadee
- **Clara**- yellow and white tabby cat, belongs to Anders and Maja, has the gift of comforting others
- **Tucker McGinty**- Irish Terrier guard dog, royal lineage, military training or so he says
- **Grendela**- grey-lag goose, protector of the girl
- **Siv**- (Seev) sturdy, dependable, and mild-tempered North Swedish horse with a deep appreciation for his keeper, Anders
- **Lottie**- landrace goat, mother of Kola, milking goat
- **Kola**- twelve-week-old kid goat

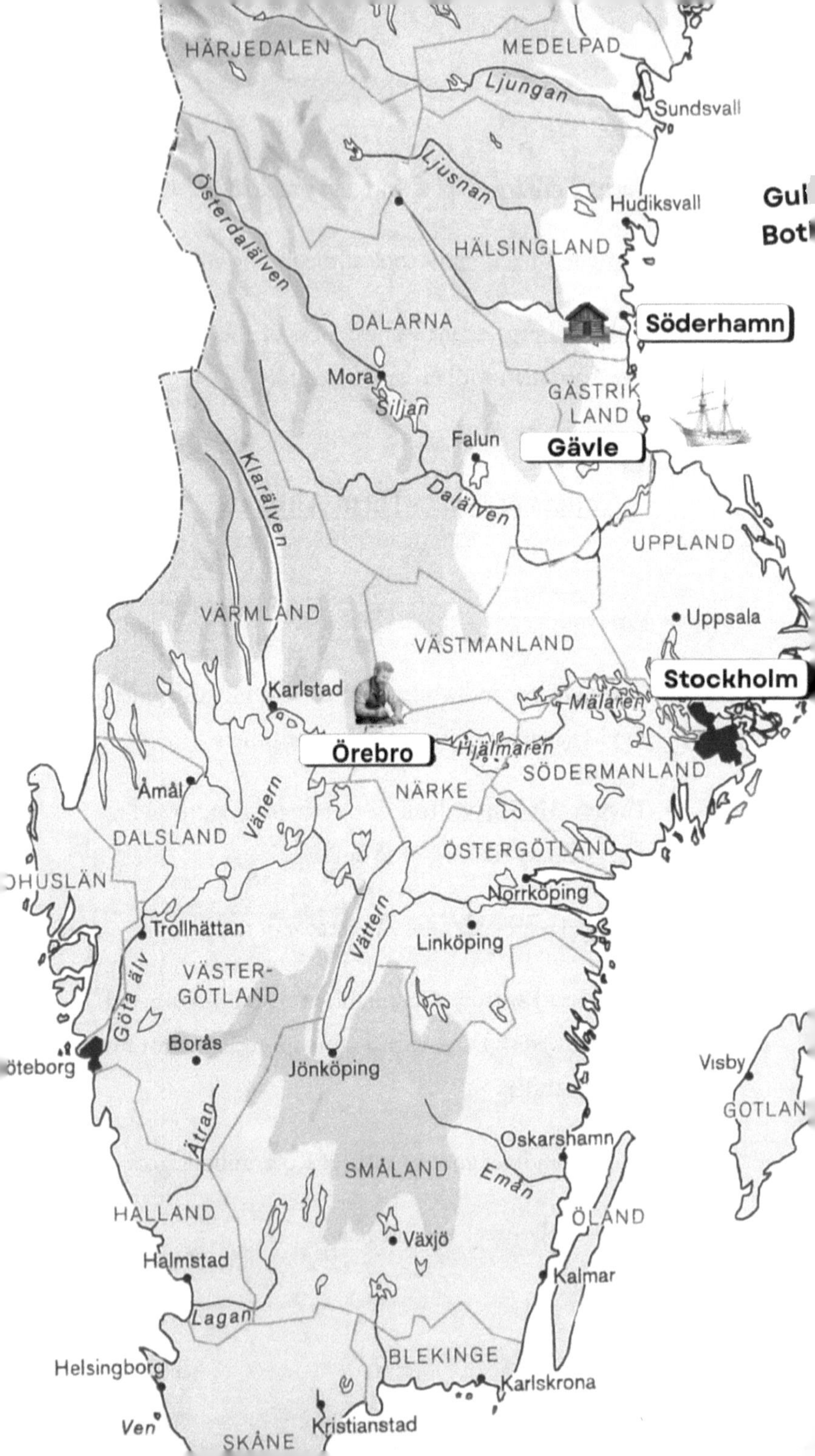

HÄRJEDALEN
MEDELPAD
Ljungan
Sundsvall
Ljusnan
Österdalälven
Hudiksvall
Gul
Bot
HÄLSINGLAND
DALARNA
Söderhamn
Mora
Siljan
GÄSTRIK
LAND
Falun
Gävle
Klarälven
Dalälven
UPPLAND
VÄRMLAND
Uppsala
VÄSTMANLAND
Stockholm
Karlstad
Mälaren
Örebro
Hjälmaren
SÖDERMANLAND
Åmål
NÄRKE
Vänern
DALSLAND
ÖSTERGÖTLAND
OHUSLÄN
Norrköping
Vättern
Trollhättan
Linköping
VÄSTER-
GÖTLAND
Göta älv
Borås
öteborg
Jönköping
Visby
GOTLAN
Ätran
Oskarshamn
SMÅLAND
Emån
HALLAND
ÖLAND
Växjö
Halmstad
Kalmar
Lagan
BLEKINGE
Helsingborg
Karlskrona
Ven
Kristianstad
SKÅNE

Swedish Words & Tucker's Sayings

Swedish Words

- **Ack!**- (Ak) Swedish term used to express a strong emotion like anger, fear, or frustration
- **Åh**- (Swedish O sound) Swedish word for "wow," short, open "a" sound such as car or father
- **Aran**- (Aaron) off-white traditional jumper (sweater) with cable patterns, knit from unscoured wool that retains its natural oils (lanolin) and makes water-resistant
- **barnauktion**- (barn-auk-shoon) historical practice in Sweden and Finland during the 19th and early 20th centuries, in which orphan and poor children were boarded out in auctions

- **Bottenviken**- (Bot-ten-vee-ken) Gulf of Bothnia, on the eastern shore of Sweden
- **Christmas julbord**- (Christmas yool-board) a buffet-style feast traditionally celebrated in Swedish culture
- **conscription**- required military service in the Swedish military
- **Dala horse**- (Dah-lah) carved horse painted bright colors, originated in Sweden
- **docka**- (dock-uh) Swedish name for doll
- **fika**- (fee-ka) cozy coffee, Swedish coffee break, coffee with ghee (cheese) and cake like an English tea
- **five-krona**- coin currency worth fifty-three cents today
- **Frau**- (Frau) Swedish translation for Mrs. or ma'am
- **galleass**- (ga-lee-es) square sail ship used for fishing in the late 1800s
- **Gävle**- (Yev-lay) Swedish town with a large group of fishermen that migrated north each year to fish and bring back to the town to sell

- **gjetost**- (yay-toast) soft cheese made from left over whey, caramel in color
- **Herr**- (Hehr) Swedish translation for Mr. or sir
- **julbröd**- (yool-brohd) braided sweet bread used as a decorative Christmas centerpiece
- **julkake bread**- (yool-kah-kah) Swedish Christmas bread used as a centerpiece for the Christmas table, made of cardamom and raisins
- **Lake Hjälmaren**- (Yel-mah-ren) fourth largest river in Sweden, 60 km long and 20 km wide, Örebro is located on the eastern edge of the lake
- **limpa bread**- (lim-puh) rye bread with caraway seeds and candied fruit
- **lutfisk**- (loo-tuh-fisk) rehydrated whitefish
- **macka**- (mac-kuh) Swedish slang term for an open sandwich
- **mandelkaka**- (man-del-kah-yoiah) Swedish almond cake, also called "visiting cake"
- **offal**- (aa-fl) cattle feed made from fish innards

- **Örebro-** (Ow-reh-bro) Swedish town situated by the Narke Plain, near lake Hjälmaren, a few kilometers inland along the Svartån River

- **pork-filled palt dumplings**- (palt) Swedish for potato—the dumplings are filled with a pork filling and topped with lingonberry jam

- **Söderhamn-** (Suh-der-hahn) Swedish town located in the northern part of Sweden along the Gulf of Bothnia

- **spitzbuben-** (shpitz-boob-ben) Swedish jam cookies dusted with powdered sugar and has a bright ruby center

- **Svartån River-** (Svahr-tohn) 100 km river that wanders through Örebro and ends in Lake Hjälmaren

Tucker's Sayings

- **c'mere to me-** come over here so I can tell you something

- **stop acting the maggot-** acting in a foolish manner

- **serious notions**- exhibiting overly zealous self-regard, boastfulness or pride

- **up and down like a fiddler's elbow**- used to describe anyone or a dog that's constantly moving for a time
- **he'd take the milk out of your tea and come back for the sugar**- describing someone who isn't trustworthy
- **has gnomes in the attic**- strange or cuckoo

Chapter 1

Karl

Karl stopped at the top of the marble staircase. He heard Sylvie reading from a book of fairy tales. Straining to hear his daughter Elia's voice, he waited by the door. After several seconds, not a whisper came from inside. Resigned to the silence, he forced himself to walk into the bedroom.

Sylvie sat in the chair beside the four-poster bed he'd slept in as a boy. Seeing him enter, she quickly wiped away tears.

He placed his hand on her shoulder. "No change today, darling?"

"No change," Sylvie replied. "Elia looks so small. Her exuberance used to fill this room. I just want it to be that way again."

"We have to believe it will be." His voice held a certainty he did not feel. "I must go now but will return soon."

Downstairs, he opened the coat closet, readying himself for a walk to town.

"How do I look?" he asked his butler, Vincent.

"Honestly, Duke, you look worn."

Blinking hard at the butler's unusual answer to his usual morning question, Karl looked in the mirror again. He'd thought he was giving off an air of calm strength.

Vincent patted Karl's shoulder. "It is to be expected, sir."

Walking toward town through wet snow, Karl replayed recent moments of the desperation that grew heavier each day. He'd attempted to hide the growing weight on his shoulders. One of a duke's duties was to be strong for others. *He could not fail in that too.*

The biting December wind blew through him, drawing him back to his task. He descended onto Örebro's snow-covered cobbled streets and took shelter in a door opening, watching bustling men in brown wool trousers and warm coats shout greetings to each other as they walked along the wooden sidewalks. Sleds of all sizes—tottering with packages, grocery items, and Christmas trees—crunched past in the hard-packed snow.

Feeling an ember of holiday joy start to warm him, Karl smiled for a moment, until his thoughts returned home. Sighing, he turned up the collar of his black woolen coat, pulled his hat down over his ears, and continued around the corner onto Estes Street.

A reverberating wail emanated from a perambulator pushed by a young mother. Klemens, the postman, stopped from his route to lean over the carriage and offer a song.

The wind is swirling, swirling round,
Whistling through streets in every town.
The wind is swirling around you and me,
Whispering, "Celebrate the newborn King."

The baby began to coo, and the mother took up the song, raising a grateful smile.

He came to earth as a wee babe.
In a manger, He was laid.

Klemens rearranged his bag of mail and crossed the street, skirting Karl. "Good morning, sir."

"Good morning, Klemens." Karl continued around the corner of Estes and Oak Street. He stopped in front of the two-story, grey-blue stone building with a black wooden sign above the door. Shuffling snow from his boots, he admired the sign's gilded lettering, *Kindberg's Wood Carving, Est. 1807.*

Equally impressive was the display in the sixteen-pane window framed with a blue valance and felted wool draperies. He passed an appreciative eye over the display's three sections: a woodland scene, a collection of various wooden toys and intricate music boxes, and his favorite, a scene showing the Christmas story.

It was an eighty-five-year-old tradition that the Kindberg family would carve wooden figures, a menagerie of animals, and several structures to tell the Christmas story from their shop window. This morning, the display's left section featured wooden carvings of Joseph standing next to a donkey carrying

Mary, the travelers resting under a tree on their journey to Bethlehem.

Karl studied each carving, enjoying the detail. The Kindberg family celebrated a long lineage of master artisans, but none as masterful as Nils.

At a sharp gust of wind, Karl shivered and walked through the door. A fire in the hearth to his right warmed the shop. The floral-patterned couch, two chairs, and small coffee table flanking the fireplace created a cozy space where the Kindbergs invited customers to have fika and share news of the town. Karl had spent many happy times enjoying coffee and cakes in front of that fire.

The smell of sawdust, oak stain, and cedar assailed his senses. He spotted Nils bent over his workbench at the back of the shop. Karl glanced over several rows of tools hanging on the wall above the bench.

His eyes settled back on Nils, who hummed as his hands deftly chiseled a small block of wood. When the wood-carver drew up short, took up a pencil, and wrote on a kraft pad of paper beside him, Karl smiled.

It was common knowledge that a story would often come to Nils about his wooden creations. Many claimed it was as if the piece was speaking to the artist as he brought it to life. Nils would always say, "The Creator is the true storyteller."

Karl cleared his throat, and Nils's tall, muscular frame turned around. A smile covered most of the wood-carver's face and lit his blue eyes. He brushed wood shavings from his sandy brown hair and then from the leather apron shielding his cream felt shirt and brown corduroy trousers.

Nils crossed the room in just a few steps, reaching out his hand. “Duke! How kind of you to stop by the shop.”

“This weather reminds me of when we were ten,” Karl said, shaking Nils’s hand, “and you were building a snow fort in front of the castle.”

Nils chuckled. “You were supposed to be helping me, but instead you were gathering ammunition.”

“Ah, yes.” Karl smirked. “I had been waiting all day for you to finish so we could have a snowball fight.”

“I believe you had the jump on me, as you did most of the time we were growing up.” Nils lowered his eyebrows angrily and then broke into a hearty laugh.

Karl laughed too. “Those were happy times, Nils.” He looked around the shop. “I see you have been busy. The store is abounding with gifts.”

“I’ve been preparing for the Christmas season all year.”

“I’m sure many families will have one of your treasures under their tree. How is your lovely wife?”

“Ah, my Rachel is well. She’s doing extra baking this year and ran out of flour, so she went to the general store to restock.”

“I can smell the mandelkaka.” Karl breathed deep, savoring the smell of toasted almonds.

“Has Stefan returned from his military duty?”

"Not yet," Nils replied. "We hope to see him soon. How's your family?"

Karl's smile weakened as despair rolled over him again. "That's what I've come about, Nils. I'm sure you have heard about my Elia."

Nils reached out to pat Karl's arm. "I have, sir, and Rachel and I have been praying for her every night. How is the wee one doing?"

"There's been little change. She continues to languish, her mother at her bedside. The doctor says he's done all he can do. Now it's up to Elia. She will need to fight."

"Oh, sir, what can I do to help?"

"Duchess Sylvie and I have attempted to buoy Elia's spirits with stories and games, but none have seemed to help. I asked the Creator what to do and He sent me to you. Would you have an idea of a creation that would draw our daughter out of her sickness?"

Nils paused, as if he was listening for something. "I don't know of one right now, but I believe the Creator will give me the exact idea your Elia will need."

Karl placed his hand on Nils's shoulder. "There are just a few weeks until Christmas. Would you be able to have the gift done by Christmas Eve?"

Nils turned and studied a bare spot on his workbench as if it held completed work. "I believe there will be more than one gift, perhaps several small pieces that will make up one larger gift. If you send Vincent to me in three days, I will give him the specifics."

"Bravo! Many days of gifts will be perfect. I will send Vincent as you request." Karl started out the door, then turned back to pump the wood-carver's hand. "Thank you, Nils."

"I'm happy to help, sir."

Rachel

Rachel quickly prepared morning fika, warming milk to put in the coffee that had been simmering on the stove. She filled a tray with cups, napkins, and two plates of mandelkaka. Tucking a loose grey hair back into the braid wound around her head, she chuckled at the sight of her apron covered with flour from baking the cake.

Just one step into the shop from their quarters at the rear allowed her to see Nils bent over his workbench. Her blue eyes met her husband's as she set the tray on the small table in front of the fire.

"As I returned with the flour, I saw the duke leaving." She tsk-tsked. "His poor Elia has been ill for quite some time. The duke's cook has been lamenting for weeks whether the girl will ever be well again. Brigitta said it seems as if the child has given up hope."

Nils sighed. "It is hard on a child to be in a bed for so long."

"It's just as hard for her parents to see her that way," Rachel responded, her voice filled with compassion. "The whole family needs some hope."

"The duke has asked me to make something to help Elia," Nils told her.

"I'll be praying the Creator guides your hands and your heart," she said, handing Nils his cake.

"Thank you, my dear. I am but a vessel."

"Yes, but a very dedicated vessel. I've seen it time and time again." Rachel placed her hand on his as they sipped their coffee.

Chapter 2

Nils

Nils held a block of grey alder, turning it over and over. He was waiting on the Creator to show him what to carve.

Each morning when Nils entered the shop, he spent time talking to the Creator, asking for His guidance and then waiting to hear direction. Sometimes it would come quickly. Other days, like today, it took longer. Nils never rushed forward. He'd learned long ago that forging ahead without direction from the Creator brought regret.

As he took another sip of coffee, Nils began to envision a figure. He quickly took up his paper and pencil as the story meant for the duke's ill daughter flowed from the Creator.

Chickadee

A cool wind brushed against my feathers and rustled the many-colored leaves on the trees.

Watch the trees closely, Father once told me. *They signal when winter will soon be upon us. Then we must do all we can to forage and cache food.*

Flying to a nearby conifer tree, I hung upside down on a branch to search for a morsel. As I was pulling a juicy bug out of the bark, a pile of seeds in a tray on a wooden pole caught my attention.

I hopped onto the branch and surveyed the area around the pile. Father's warning about predators went off in my mind. Only ninety-two days old, I took his advice seriously and flew past the tray several times, but there was no movement. I went through Father's checklist: cats, birds of prey, humans. None of those predators to be seen, I slowly flitted down to the tray.

It held a generous amount of pine, cypress, and fir seeds, along with juicy juniper berries. I began carrying them one by one to my new cache, a knothole high in a conifer tree.

After several trips, I stopped to nibble on a pine seed and, out of the corner of my eye, spotted a woodsman carrying an axe and a tin pail. The ruddy-faced man had blue eyes, light brown hair, and a long beard. His muslin shirt fit tightly over his thick arms. A long burgundy overcoat with cream-colored buttons partially covered his brown breeches and leather boots.

He was less than twenty yards from me and looked right at where I sat on the platform. I went entirely still. A tactic I practiced over and over with Father before venturing out on my own.

Father's words came back to me. You must blend into the background when a predator approaches. Be still, so it is hard for them to see you.

"Hey, little bird," the woodsman said, staring at me. "Are you hungry? I have plenty here for you." He placed his axe next to a chair at the front of the cabin, pulled off his gloves, and retrieved several pine cones from his pocket, holding the cones in his calloused hands.

Oh no! The seeds I'd been taking were his! I had to get away before he punished me, so I flew to the top of a nearby conifer.

"You don't have to go, little bird. I gather a few cones and seeds as I'm cutting wood around Söderhamn. I add them to the tray, a small offering to help my feathered friends survive our winters." As the woodsman explained, his voice was filled with gentle understanding.

I flitted to a nearby branch. Was he luring me closer so he could capture me? His quiet demeanor and my own sense of adventure gave me the courage to try grabbing seeds again.

This time, I snatched two seeds and sat in a tree, watching the woodsman as he brought out another handful of seeds for the tray.

"Take all you need, little one. There's plenty for you."

I descended as if to take a cypress seed. But a rustling in the bushes diverted me to the top of the roof. The woodsman must've heard the rustling too, because he started toward the bushes.

"Hello?" he called as he walked nearer the location of the sound. "Is someone there?"

There was a whimper, then movement again.

I flew to the branch above the bush and saw a wisp of a girl with red plaited hair. Her tear-stained face and filthy clothes were a stark contrast to her delicate white skin and grey-blue eyes. A swath of freckles covered her face across the middle. She wore burgundy mittens and a tattered grey woolen coat, a burgundy skirt, and a striped pinafore. Her boots were fur, and the dark stockings meant to cover her legs had a hole in one knee.

The woodsman bent down by the bush, pulled back the green foliage, and was taken aback. "Well, hello, little one! What are you doing in the bushes?"

The girl spoke so softly I could barely hear her. "Please sir, since you feed the birds, may I have something to eat too?"

In the girl's eyes was a distressing pain no one so young should know, and her body trembled. Her fear was so palpable it was impossible not to feel a surge of empathy. I wanted to assure her that the woodsman was someone she could trust. He had not hurt me even after I took his seeds.

The woodsman stepped back and spoke tenderly. "Of course you may."

He offered the girl his hand as if to help her stand, but she pulled back sharply. The woodsman gave a gentle smile and turned toward the cabin, walking slowly to allow the girl to follow.

At the cabin, he moved his axe away from the whitewashed wooden chair to the left of the door. "You may sit here on this chair, and I will bring you something to eat."

After the woodsman entered the cabin, the hungry girl stood by the chair, her eyes darting fearfully.

I returned to the feeder and again plucked a conifer seed from the tray.

The woodsman soon returned with a plate of food—a piece of hard cheese and a slice of rye bread spread with butter.

"Here you go child." The woodsman tried to hand the plate to her, but she stepped backward.

"I will put this on the chair for you," he said softly, "and get you some milk."

After he stepped back into the cabin, the girl looked around furtively, creeping up to the chair. She grabbed the bread and cheese from the plate and ran back into the bushes.

I wondered what could make such a wee girl so afraid. Did she, too, have predators after her?

The woodsman returned with a tin cup of milk and found the plate and the yard empty. "Please come back," he called. "I have milk for you."

There was no answer. He placed the cup of milk on the chair and peered through the bushes but did not find the wee girl.

A familiar dee-dee, my mother's call, came from the grove of trees near my home. I swiftly plucked a juniper berry and took flight.

"Goodbye, little bird," the woodsman said as he began combing the woods beside the cabin. "Do come back again."

Nils

Nils finished writing the last line of the story, then picked up his chisel. He whittled away to form first a round body, next a head, and finally feet. Using a small V-tool, he pressed with precision along the sides of the body to add lines for the wings, eyes, and sides of the beak.

After a few hours, the work table was covered with wood shavings, in their center, a chickadee holding a tiny juniper berry in its beak. Dusting off the carving with a brush, Nils laughed.

"You are a hungry fellow, aren't you?"

Clearing off the work surface, he laid out a scrap of cotton fabric, placed the carving on it, and pulled out his stains and paints. The warm hue of the grey alder wood made a perfect base for the grey-headed chickadee.

Nils painstakingly added a dark brown cap to the head, then more of the same color under the beak and around the eyes. With careful precision, he painted black on the beak, eyes, feet, and wings. He added a white strip on each side of the head and on the bird's breast, then white shadowing on the wings.

Once the dark brown cap was dry, he used a dry brush to apply a greyish-brown stain in the lines along the cap. Nils finished off the chickadee with a mixture of medium brown and warm red draped over the top of the wings like a shawl and bringing the back and sides of the body to life. The stem held in the bird's mouth received a greenish-brown coloring, and each blue-painted juniper berry sported a white dot.

"There you are, my little bird, in all your glory. Tomorrow, once you're completely dry, I'll give you a couple of wax coats." Nils closed up his paints.

"Dinner is ready, my dear," Rachel called from the kitchen.

"Good night, little bird," Nils said. "It's time for my supper. Soon, you'll be off to the castle to tell your story and, hopefully, give Elia the courage to fight through her fever."

Chapter 3

Vincent

Vincent tucked his scarf into his woolen coat as the biting, icy wind from Lake Hjälmaren blew through the streets of Örebro. With its decorated homes, the town was a picture of winter charm, contrasting the sorrow back at the castle.

He had attempted to cheer Elia with a show of shadow puppets before he left, but she barely stayed awake long enough to see the bunny bouncing through the field. The trial of sickness had recently visited many homes in Örebro, but Elia had been ill the longest.

Stepping up onto the wooden sidewalk, Vincent noticed the pastor's children, a young boy and girl waiting patiently on a bench outside the general store. The pastor's wife was talking with the store clerk. He greeted both women and sat next to the children. “What are you two fine youngsters doing today?”

The small boy hid behind the taller girl as if for protection.

“We’re helping our mother with the shopping,” the girl said shyly, looking at Vincent’s clothes. All were grey except for his black leather boots, which had been polished to a shine. “Do you work at the castle?”

“I do,” Vincent said, smiling. “I have worked there all my life, and my father worked for the Vasa family before me. My name is—”

A shrill squeal interrupted him from across the street, and a raucous boy came running toward the bench.

“Herr Vincent, Herr Vincent!” the boy yelled, stopping short before them.

“Hello, Arne!” Vincent chuckled. “What are you up to today?”

“I am running errands for my ma. I had to come tell you. Christmas is coming soon, and Ma said I can put the Swedish flags on the tree this year all by myself.”

“Well, well. That is quite a responsibility. I think you deserve a treat.” Vincent reached into his coat pocket, then handed Arne a piece of white-and-red taffy.

“Oh, åh! Thanks so much, Herr Vincent! I have more errands to run so I best get going.” Arne darted across the street. He turned around to shout back “Merry Christmas!” and then ran out of sight.

The young girl and her brother stared after Arne. Vincent reached into his pocket again and pulled out two more pieces of taffy.

"Patient children deserve a treat," he said, giving the young girl both pieces, as her brother eyed him bashfully from behind her.

"Thank you, Herr Vincent," she said, handing one piece of candy to her brother, "from both of us."

"You're welcome." He stood up to leave and waved at the children, his heart feeling light. His butler position forced him to be formal and sometimes stern, but the town's children allowed him to be informal and, at times, exuberant. When he heard their squeals of delight as he pulled sweets from his pocket stash, it brought him a great sense of joy.

The cuckoo clock struck ten when Vincent arrived at Kindberg's shop.

"My old friend, I'm happy to see you," Nils said as Vincent entered.

"I am happy to see you as well." Vincent shook Nils's hand. "I hear you have a treasure for our Elia."

"Yes!" Nils nodded to a small blue muslin bag tied with a white ribbon. "Rachel has made a special bag for the gift. A child who has such a struggle is dear to her heart after our Stefan was so sick with colic as a baby."

"I'm sure that's so." Vincent pulled a tiny scroll tied with string from the bag and smiled. "Ah, I see the story has come with this one. I pray it will help the girl to feel better."

"As do I," said Nils.

"I'll return to town at the end of the week," Vincent told him. "Would you like me to stop by and see if you have another treasure ready?"

"Yes, I am working on the second piece now."

Rachel emerged from the Kindbergs' living quarters with a serving tray. "I knew that voice the minute I heard you, so I put on the kettle for coffee and brought out some spitzbuben."

Vincent greedily eyed the contents of the tray, golden-brown star cookies with centers of red currant jam. "I've never been able to resist your spitzbuben, but I can only stay for one cup of your delicious coffee. I have several other errands to tend to before returning to the castle."

The threesome sat around the table in front of the fire, catching up on news of the town, family, and friends. When his cup was empty, Vincent noticed through the display window that snow had begun falling.

"I'd best be going!" He tucked the bag with Elia's gift inside his coat pocket. "I still need to pick up items from the butcher and the weaver."

Rachel handed him a small box. "Here is a bit of spitzbuben to take home. Tell your dear wife that she is welcome to visit anytime. It has been so long since we've all been able to get together for a chat."

"I will let her know," Vincent said, lifting the treat box high with a smile as he exited the door.

His coat soon wet with snow, he shivered as he finished his errands. A few yards from the castle, the wind gusted and attempted to carry off his hat, and he rushed with his packages to get across the drawbridge.

Shaking the snow off his coat, he felt a rush of warmth as he entered the kitchen, where his wife stood washing vegetables in the sink.

"Brrr, the snow is really coming down now," he told her.

"I'm glad you made it back before it got even worse," Brigitta responded. "Put your coat and hat by the fire here. The duchess was just down asking if you had returned. She is waiting for you in the morning room."

Vincent handed Brigitta the box of cookies. "A gift from Rachel. She hopes you will visit soon."

"That was so thoughtful of her, but I'm not sure any of us but you can be spared from the castle with the child so sick." Brigitta sighed.

Vincent wound through the downstairs office and storage rooms, up a flight of stairs and to a hallway lined with family portraits of the Vasa family, and to the morning room. Several east-facing windows flooded the sage-green room with warmth until midday. The duchess was bent over a small desk in the corner, her golden hair braided into a long plait, entwined with a soft pink ribbon that matched her gown.

"M'lady, I have returned with the gift."

"Oh, Vincent! I'm glad you returned before the storm grew worse." She drew a carved chickadee from the bag he gave her and smiled, eyeing the bird from all sides.

"Nils is a talented man and is indeed inspired by the Creator. I pray that this is enough to help Elia through this dark time." Her voice broke.

"We are all praying, Ma'am."

"I know, Vincent." Duchess Sylvie left the room with her head bowed.

Sylvie

As she climbed the stairs to the third story, Sylvie considered the loyalty of the castle's servants, especially Vincent. As the years progressed, his short blond hair was starting to grey around his temples. But his cornflower-blue eyes, prominent nose, and dimpled chin remained as steadfast as he was in character.

She opened Elia's door gently and saw her husband stroking their daughter's hand and singing her a lullaby. Sylvie's heart wrenched. This trial was hard on Karl too. She lifted a quiet prayer for strength for both of them.

"Darling," she said as she approached the bed. "Vincent has returned with the carving from Nils."

Karl turned to her, his eyes brightening. He took the bag from her and spoke to the small form in the bed. "Elia, we have a surprise for you. Carver Kindberg has made something just for you."

The young girl's eyes fluttered open as the duchess helped her sit up by adding another pillow behind her.

Karl opened the bag, handing his wife the scroll and holding the bag open for Elia.

Elia looked but didn't reach inside. Karl took out the carving.

"Look at this hungry bird," he said, turning the piece around.

Elia looked at the carving, but soon her eyes closed.

"I'm sure you are tired, my dear," Sylvie said. "Let me read you the story of this little bird."

She unrolled the scroll and began to read. Twice, a smile appeared on her daughter's face, but Elia was softly snoring when Sylvie finished reading.

"Our little one has fallen asleep," Karl said.

"Yes, she is still very weak. I will put the bird on her bedside table so she can see it when she wakes." Tears welled up in Sylvie's eyes. "Oh, Karl, I do hope this encouragement helps."

Karl put his arm around her. "So do I, my dear. So do I.

Chapter 4

Clara

"A tabby cat can make anyone feel loved," my woodsman said, scratching between my ears. He stopped scratching and wrapped a chunk of cheese and two pieces of buttered rye bread in a checkered cloth, depositing the bundle and a cup of milk in a tin box on the wooden chair in front of the cabin.

"Will you watch for her, Clara?" He closed the box's lid.

You can count on me, I thought. He'd told me about the red-haired girl who came for food. *If she comes again, I will make her feel welcome.*

"I have just one more order of wood to fill this week for the Von Bahrs. Thankfully, even though many are installing some sort of electricity in Söderhamn, most cooks still prefer to have wooden stoves to make their meals." My woodsman grabbed his axe and headed off into the woods.

The days were getting shorter and shorter, and leaves fluttered from the trees in a downward dance, dipping and swirling to the forest floor, designing a patchwork quilt of red, yellow, and orange. In the distance, woodpeckers drummed through the bark of dead trees, and squirrels ran up and down live trunks, gathering acorns.

I settled near the weathered wooden chair, lost in thoughts about the girl who came by for food and then about my own journey to this cabin.

As a kitten, I often felt out of place in my litter of five. All my siblings shared the same calico coloring as our mother, while I was plain yellow and white. I couldn't help but feel different, like I didn't quite belong.

"Darling, yellow tabby cats are like sunshine," Mother reassured me. "They are very special. You will see."

As we grew up, I found those words a great comfort, especially as each of my siblings showed their prowess on the farm while I struggled to even catch a mouse. After yet another failed attempt to corner a wily vermin, my mother sat me down.

"Let me tell you a story about Frau Ackerman, the farmer's wife. About a month after arriving with her husband here at the farm, she found a tiny yellow-and-white tabby abandoned in the forest. Frau Ackerman had lived in the city of Söderhamn and found farm life to be very lonely. She named her new cat, Freya.

"Grandma Freya was her cat?"

"Yes. Grandma Freya kept her new owner company on long days when Herr Ackerman was farming." Mother's voice filled with love as she purred and licked my coat. You're so like Grandma Freya, meant to bring joy to those around you. What a wonderful gift you will be."

Not long after that, the Ackermans' woodcutter neighbor, Herr Dahl, delivered wood to the farm. Mother overheard him ask Frau Ackerman if she might have an extra cat he could gift his wife. She had been grieving the loss of their infant son, who had lived only a few days.

"Oh, I have just the kitten for you, Herr Dahl." Frau Ackerman pointed me out in the barn. "She looks like my Freya."

"That is uncanny," Herr Dahl mused. "She looks exactly like her."

"See, my dear," Mother said as she nudged me forward. "Now is the time for you to be a ray of sunshine."

Herr Dahl wrapped me in his coat, and we began our journey back to his cabin. The wind rustled through the trees, and I could feel the warmth of his woodsman's coat against my fur. As we approached the cabin, he placed me on this same chair outside the front door and went inside.

I thought the place would do very well for my new home, until a reddish-brown terrier growled at me as he rounded the corner of the cabin. "Who are you? You've no permission to be here."

"Yes, I do," I said. "I was brought here by the man that went in the cabin."

"That's news to me!" the dog sputtered, looking me up and down. "Well, if that is the way it is to be, c'mere to me and I will tell you the rules of the place."

Ignoring him, I stayed seated on the chair.

"I am Tucker McGinty," he began anyway, "and I come from a long line of Irish nobility. Rightly so, I'm the leader of this farm. There are rules for every animal here, and I enforce those rules."

I lay down on the chair, then began to lick my paws to show disinterest in his blustering.

"First," he continued, "you are only allowed in the barn area behind the cabin, which I will show you when I am ready. Second, do not go in the cabin or approach the humans without permission from me. Third, since you are the lowest rank in the regiment, you will eat last."

At number four in his pompous list, I leapt down from the chair and started toward the barn, showing my complete disregard for his highness's rules.

"Are you listening to me?" he demanded.

"No," I said as I ventured on a worn path that curved around the side of the cabin to a barn. The four stalls inside on the left had half doors and wooden latches. Two horses, a cow, and several goats lived there. On the right were mounds of hay and tools. In a small chicken coop beside the barn, a black-and-red rooster guarded several Swedish flower hens, all sporting colorful plumage and scratching and pecking the dirt.

Apparently, Tucker had found it necessary to follow me. His incessant barking about rules and his "rightful place on the farm" scared the chickens, and they tottered into the cover of the coop.

I strolled back to the thick wooden door at the front of the cabin. It was open, so I sashayed in.

"You cannot go in there!" Tucker barked, repeating himself incessantly.

My woodsman was bent over the stone hearth, grabbing the kettle of coffee and pouring himself a cup. He smiled when he saw me enter. I looked back at Tucker with a smirk.

"Quiet, Tucker," my woodsman said as he closed the door, Tucker still standing outside.

Tucker continued to bark, something like "This is not over! Blah, blah, blah. My rules something, something, something."

I grinned as I looked around the one-room cabin. It was small but tidy, with gingham curtains on the two windows. To the upper right was a bedroom loft, on the left wall a large stone fireplace with two chairs in front.

A woman was mending a pair of breeches in the rocking chair. She was willowy, with golden hair and pale blue eyes that seemed to hold a profound sadness. She stopped rocking as I entered.

"What is *this*, Anders?" she asked.

"I thought we needed a cat, Maja," he said, "mostly to keep down the mice."

I walked over to her and began to rub against her legs.

"She's not shy," Maja said.

"That she is not," Anders mused. "Frau Ackerman said she is like her Freya, a ray of sunshine. I think we could both use some of that." His voice broke. "So I brought her home."

I jumped up on my new mistress's lap, purring with joy. Maja began petting my head as Anders watched from the table.

"Frau Ackerman knows her cats," Maja said slowly, a small smile forming on her lips. "She raves about Freya all the time. I think we should call this one Clara."

"Whatever you want, my dear." He smiled as he walked to the door of the cabin. "She's a gift for you."

Tucker McGinty returned to his rant as soon as the door opened. Anders shooed him away and closed the door behind them. To the sound of Tucker barking his disdain, I curled up in Maja's lap to nap.

Yes, I thought back then. *This home will do very well.*

Now a full-grown cat tempted to nap all day in the weathered chair, I kept myself alert by considering uncountable evenings spent with Maja and Anders as he reads stories from a book about rebellious people and the Father who still loved them. Maja and Anders loved me and even Tucker McGinty that way. Perhaps the girl who came by for food needed to experience that love, I decided I would watch for her all day every day.

Each morning, Anders placed another serving of food in the box, charging me to watch over it. When he came home with his wagon full of wood, he checked the box, sighed, and handed Tucker and me the milk and food.

"I wish I knew where the lass came from," he said on the third day. "I've checked with everyone in Söderhamn, and no one knows who she is. We'll just have to wait and see if she returns."

After the fourth day, I thought Anders would surely give up on the routine. But he filled the tin again each day following.

On the seventh day, while Anders was in the barn, I saw a wisp of red hair behind the thicket of black currants. I licked my paws intently, acting like I didn't see the girl.

She crept step by step to the chair, eyes darting to the right and then to the left. Once she reached the chair, she picked up the cup, drank the milk in one gulp, and then grabbed the food.

I strolled her way to welcome her, but she ran off before I could even rub up against her leg.

Moments later, Anders came around the corner of the cabin and noticed the empty tin. He asked me, "Clara, did you see our young friend when she came to get the food?"

"I did, I did!" I told him. "I tried to tell the girl you would help her, but she ran off before I could even mew a word." I repeated my story, but as is often the case with animal and human communication, I'm sure all Anders heard was *meow, meow, meow.*

"I know, Clara," he responded. "I know. The girl is very frightened. One step at a time my furry friend. Maybe, once Maja returns, she will be able to talk with the girl." He took a drink of water from the pail. "The wee lass needs us, so we will take our time in letting her know this is a safe place."

Chapter 5

Nils

Nils waved goodbye to Vincent through the store's front window, happy his second creation was on its way to Elia. He folded his arms and watched Rachel dust each carving in the window display. Her industriousness took him back to the first year they moved into the shop. Cleaning the display had been Nils's job as his father's apprentice, but Rachel took it over until their son became old enough to take on the task. "I don't think I know anyone who enjoys cleaning as much as you do, dear wife."

"Stefan isn't here to help, so I am filling up the window in his stead." She moved Joseph, Mary, and the donkey closer to the town and added a few animals around the manger. "Don't you think it strange we have not heard from our son?"

Nils had heard Rachel's prayers to the Creator for the last few nights. As days passed with no word from Stefan, she was becoming more and more concerned. "It has been a busy Christmas season without his help in the shop," Nils said, "but he had his duty to serve since he is now a grown man."

Rachel sighed. "If only we knew where he was. All the rest of the young men arrived back from conscription a week ago. I spoke to Frau Edlund's son at the market, but he hadn't seen Stefan since all the boys were discharged. Stefan had planned to come home with the rest of them but was not at the train station when the others arrived. This lack of communication is not like him. What if he is hurt or worse?"

"You have prayed, and so have I," Nils said, cupping her chin in his hand. "We know the Creator hears our prayers, so He is watching over Stefan. I'm sure we would've heard by now if something was wrong."

"You're right," she said. "I need to focus on getting ready for Christmas." Returning to her work at the window, she placed three shepherds and a flock of sheep to the right of Bethlehem. "Tend to your flock well, shepherds. Soon you will receive great news!" She tucked the edges of the velvet curtain behind hooks on each side of the window display.

Nils surveyed the brightly colored ornaments of paper and straw hanging throughout the shop. Candles flickered on the mantle, and a tray laden with cookies sat on the table in front of the fireplace. "We're eight days from Christmas, and you already have the store full of holiday cheer."

Rachel handed him the empty box of Christmas carvings. "Speaking of cheer, I need to get back to the kitchen to make another batch of candles."

"Another batch?" Nils swept sawdust off the workbench. "How many is that now?"

"Five," she said.

"Five!" He laughed. "We will have enough light for the entire year if you keep going."

"I may have enough wax for six batches if I'm thrifty. I'll add several candles to the Modine family's holiday basket, as well as baked goods, knitted woolen socks, and decoration supplies. Helping the Modines is doubly important this Christmas. Fionda has been taking in seamstress work, but with her four little ones and Charles's medical bills . . . I thought I could help out."

"Herr Sten feels terrible that Charles broke his leg delivering grain to his farm. Thankfully, Charles will heal and be able to return to work in time." Nils put his arm around Rachel. "Your heart for others is just another reminder of how blessed I am to have you as my wife."

She sank into his chest. "Both of us have special projects this holiday season to help show the love of the Creator."

"Indeed! I have Herr Orrell's jewelry box to finish." Nils picked up a piece of sandpaper and began buffing the corners of the box. "Then I'll begin on another character in the story the Creator is weaving for Elia."

Vincent

Vincent hurried back to the castle and found the duke stooping over his desk in the study. Sunlight flowing through the two floor-to-ceiling windows flanked by dark green draperies warmed the room's stone walls. A fire crackling in the hearth released the sweet smell of apple wood. Vincent knocked as he entered.

"Back already, Vincent?" The duke returned his quill to the inkwell.

Vincent handed the bag he carried to the duke. "Nils had the gift ready—a sweet yellow kitty I think will bring a smile to her face."

The duke peered into the bag. "And another scroll?"

Vincent nodded. "I asked Nils if the stories that accompany the carvings come to him in pieces or as a whole. He told me both, they come to him in many different ways but were always a gift from the Creator. When I mentioned the stories seem so real, he said he's wondered too if they are like the Bible, based on someone's life. Either way, he's as excited as we are to hear the rest of the tale the Creator has for Elia."

Smiling, the duke carefully placed his account book into a drawer and rose from his desk. "I will take it to her. Thank you, Vincent."

"My pleasure!" said Vincent as he walked out of the study.

Karl

Karl found Duchess Sylvie sitting in one of the two wingback chairs near Elia's four-poster bed. Every time he walked into that bedroom, he remembered the place that had been his childhood sanctuary adorned in dark blue and hunter green. Thinking of the countless hours he and his younger brother had spent playing there with their rock collections, games, and tin soldiers brought a warm smile to his face.

The room was much different now. Passing the soft blue draperies, Karl picked up Elia's doll Tova from a small table with two matching chairs and nestled the doll under the cream bedspread beside his daughter. He sighed deeply, missing the echo of Elia's laughter off the stone walls as she ran down the hallways. The castle was somberly quiet, as if its heart also broke at seeing Elia lay lifeless in her bed.

Consciously trying to shake off his melancholy, Karl donned a smile and drew the other wingback chair close to Sylvie's. "Look, my darling, another gift from Nils."

She smiled warmly at him as he opened the muslin bag, handed her the scroll, and pulled out the carving.

“Look at this soft yellow color Nils has used,” Karl said, rubbing his thumb over the slight grooves along the cat’s body. “And white tips on all four paws.”

“The pink nose and white whiskers make it so charming,” Sylvie said, “as if it will meow at any moment.” She unrolled the scroll and read the first lines on it to herself. “Well, well. This carving has a name. Clara. That’s surprising, since the chickadee did not come with a name.”

“His name is Pip,” Elia said in a soft voice.

Karl jumped to stand beside the bed, placing his hand on Elia’s. “I did not mean to wake you, my dear. What did you say?”

“The bird’s name is Pip,” Elia said a bit louder.

“Pip,” Sylvie repeated. “That’s a funny name.”

“I named him the first day,” Elia said, her eyes slowly opening. “He is but a pip of a bird. Small but courageous.” Reaching for the bird on her side table, she snuggled it to her chest and soon fell back asleep.

Karl smiled at his wife as he continued to hold Elia’s hand. He gazed at their daughter, a tiny flicker of warmth and hope flooding his being.

“When you told me the Creator directed you to go to the wood-carver for help,” Sylvie said, her voice shaking with emotion, “I thought, *What could he do? He isn’t a doctor.* I should have known the Creator works in ways we don’t understand.”

"I knew the physician had done all he could," Karl said as they both watched Elia sleep. "Only the Creator could help Elia. I, too, had my doubts about the method, but I'm glad I listened."

She lowered her voice to a whisper. "I can't wait to see what the Creator inspires Nils to make next."

"And what happens in the story the Father is telling us," Karl added.

Chapter 6

Tucker

"Did you see her, Tuck?" Clara asked me.

"My name is not Tuck," I told her for the twentieth time that day. "It is Tucker McGinty."

"Yeah, yeah, I know. You're from a royal line of Irish terriers bred for military operations and used especially for tracking. I've heard it a thousand times. Did you see the girl who came for food?"

For the past three weeks, I had diligently patrolled the property line, ensuring no intruders crossed. As my master's loyal guard dog for six years, I'd never missed a trespasser. But this infernal girl had managed to evade my watchful eyes. Determined not to let her sneak up on me again, I increased my patrols, making multiple turns around the farm daily.

"My perimeter check found no intruders, but I will spot her the next time she comes around."

"We will see," Clara said, smirking while she licked her paw. "I am sure Anders will be laying out food for her again today."

"I will be the first to notice her approaching," I assured the cat. "My keen sense of smell picks up a scent a mile away."

"Not if you're taking a nap like you were the last couple of times the girl appeared." Clara chuckled.

"Humph! It's lucky for her that I didn't catch her last time. I would've scared her silly with my growl and fierceness."

"Down boy," Clara mewed. "The wee girl already has such fear in her eyes. We have been ordered to welcome her."

"Anyone sneaking onto this property is getting barked at," I declared staunchly. "No exceptions. It's my duty to protect this place."

I took another turn around the perimeter and then returned to my bowl next to the cabin's door to eat my breakfast.

Anders came out with food and a cup, set them in the tin box on the chair, and instructed Clara to watch out for the red-haired girl. Once he went back inside to finish cleaning up after breakfast, a curious scent floated in on the breeze. My hair rose on end, and I gave out a low growl.

"Settle down, Tucker McGinty!" Anders said sternly from the other side of the open cabin door. "I do not want you scaring the wee girl."

Settle down? I thought. *Doesn't he know my job is to protect the property?*

"I want you to follow her," he whispered. "Not so close she will see you, but find out where she goes."

Ah, yes! Reconnaissance.

"Absolutely sir," I said. "I'm the right dog for the job. I'll track her and report back." Sadly, as is often the case with communication between guard dog and master, I'm certain all Anders heard was *bark, bark, bark*.

Anders began to hum a tune, wrapped his scarf around his throat, and grabbed his axe as he came out the door. He continued around the corner of the cabin, out of sight.

To my right, a bit of red hair and two blue eyes peeked around a hazel bush.

"The intruder has been spotted," I said covertly to Clara. The silly cat acted like she didn't hear me, so I repeated my announcement.

"I heard you the first time, dog," she hissed. "I'm acting as if we don't see her."

"Oh," I said quietly, lying down on the step and watching the wee girl creep up to the door and open the tin. That infernal cat was wrapped around the girl's legs before I could even act. The girl reached down to pet her.

Not to be outdone, I slowly approached the girl and stood in my regal pose, head held high, legs firmly in a rectangle, body ramrod straight. Sure, I was a sight to behold. I toned my bark down to a woof so I wouldn't scare her.

"Hi, puppy! How are you?"

Puppy? I'm not a puppy! Do humans not know the difference? I began to growl in my frustration.

Clara snickered. "Tone it down, *puppy*. Remember what Anders said. I thought you were good at taking orders, since you were trained to do military operations."

"Stop acting the maggot, cat," I retorted. "I excel in all I do." I got hold of myself and began rolling on the ground to expose my underside. I would show that cat who was the best soldier.

The girl began scratching my belly. Humans seem to love doing that.

I heard a faint calling from the woods that only my ears could pick up since it was some distance away. It repeated several times before the girl noticed, took the food from the tin box on the chair, and ran back into the bushes, leaving the full cup of milk behind.

I jumped up and shook the dirt from my reddish-brown fur. "Well, Clara, I'm now off on my highly important mission. I will find out where the girl goes." I paused to make sure I'd been heard.

"Well, you better get going, as she is a quick one, that wee girl." Clara went around a corner of the cabin before I could explain how I would achieve the feat before me with my stellar agility and tracking skills.

Honestly, I was soon surprised by the girl's ability to maneuver so quickly through the forest landscape. I sensed she had been on this trail before, and although I lost sight of her several times, my keen smelling ability always found her again.

At times, I had to fall back so she couldn't see me as she wound through clumps of underbrush and over a stream. Puffing from the exertion, the wee girl stooped over to catch her breath. Then she stepped into a mass of bushes and pulled out a sled stacked with small sticks and branches, frantically picking up and adding more twigs.

Once again, she was on the move. She burst into a clearing I recognized as the coastline of the Gulf of Bothnia, called Bottenviken by the locals. Anchored in the freshwater bay there was a galleass with square sails.

It looks like a Gävle fishery, I deduced from traveling with Anders to fishing villages to sell wood. *That is where the wee girl lives. I will have to tell Anders.*

To gather more intel, I skirted the woods closer to shore, where several twenty-four-foot rowboats made of spruce and twisted wood dotted the bay, their nets lowered. I made my way between two boats on shore.

There were shouts out on the water, so I ducked out of sight and watched as the boats rowed into a circle. They must have found a school of herring. The boats tightened the circle and soon were hauling in a large catch.

I watched for a bit and then grabbed a herring that had fallen out of a boat onto the shore. Continuing my reconnaissance, I darted back into the woods, dropping the fish in a safe place before heading off to check out the rest of the fishing camp. Once I was farther inshore, I checked for any humans and then slunk behind a row of shanties painted a dull grey. They seemed to be empty, so I belly-crawled to the barn, where I found goats, sheep, and two pigs.

A metallic clanging sound caught my attention, so I stealthily approached a small hut where a man inside was pounding a piece of metal into a ring. Picking up a piece of wood, he planed it to the same size as several pieces lying on his bench. I could smell pine in the salty air as shavings fell to the ground. Taking the two metal rings, the man began to methodically place the wooden boards in a circle, forming the outside of a barrel.

Back toward shore, I observed the girl straining to pull her full sled up to a large pot over a fire. A grey-haired humpbacked man stirred something in the pot. The girl's arms shook after she dropped the rope.

"Where've you been, girl?" he yelled. "It doesn't take that long to gather firewood."

"I have to go farther into the woods to get the sticks now, as we have been using so many." She set about unloading the sled.

"Ack!" the man exclaimed. "That's not going to be enough! The others will be in soon, and the soup is not done. More wood, you lazy girl! Or you'll get no food again today." He spat on the ground.

"Y-yes, sir."

"Go and be quick about it!" he hollered.

The girl ran back to the woods, tears streaming down her face.

Did I hear right? Were they not feeding the girl?

Staying out of sight, I watched a large man get out of a rowboat at the shoreline. His outfit was the same as most fishermen—woolen trousers, an Aran sweater under a raincoat, rubber boots, and a stocking hat. However, his sizable frame wasn't like the fishermen I'd seen before. This man had a thick neck, large battered hands, and a stern face. His eyes were clear blue, but there was no life in them. Dull and mean, they made me shiver despite my nerves of steel.

The fisherman strode toward the pot over the fire.

"Where's the runt?" he bellowed.

"Here," the lass said, tottering back with another armload of wood.

"Get these fish guts in the barrels of brine quick-like," he said, kicking several buckets. "I need them salted so I can sell the offal to locals for their cattle."

The wee lass picked up a bucket in each hand. Trying to move swiftly, she stumbled and spilled half of one bucket.

“Again, you miserable runt?” the man roared. “You cost me every time I turn around. For that, you’ll be without supper tonight.”

“Please, I didn’t have supper last night!” The wee girl sobbed.

“Don’t talk back to me! Do as you’re told.” The man turned his back on her.

This poor girl! I thought. *No wonder she is so hungry. I must get back to Anders and somehow let him know her situation.*

Chapter 7

Nils

The fire was a symphony of pops and cracklings. Nils could smell the warm, sugary aromas of spiced bread baking in the oven as he bent over his workbench. Looking out the window, he glimpsed snowflakes softly falling and townspeople opening stores, piling deliveries on sleds, and brushing snow off the wooden sidewalks.

As Christmas drew near, the town was alive with the buzz of anticipation. The holiday season meant home-cooked food, weeks of celebration, and the beauty of Advent. Every day was filled with a joyful frenzy—people humming tunes, exchanging pleasantries with their neighbors, and eagerly seeking the perfect gift.

Ah, the perfect gift. Nils pondered the concept. *Only one Gift is truly special*. He turned the wooden carving in his hand over and over. *Hopefully the girl in the woodsman's story will discover Him.*

"Well, Tucker McGinty," the wood-carver said, "I will attempt to make you with great military bearing." Nils moved his chisel with precision as he rounded the dog's tail. He edged lines on the canine's face, each stroke revealing the wiry coat and beard. Brushing off the sawdust, he checked that the grooves were the correct depth.

"Now to your floppy ears. Then I'll be ready to paint your red, wheaten-colored coat." Nils studied his subject and chuckled. "I believe I will add touches of cream in your eyebrows and beard to show what a seasoned soldier you are."

Nils continued to ardently work on the wooden terrier—his thoughts drifting to the story that inspired this sentinel of a dog—until Rachel appeared in the shop with a large wooden box of carvings.

"Here, my dear. Let me help you." Nils took the box from her with a warm smile. "You know, I always enjoy moments when we work together."

"Oh, thank you," she said, smiling up at him. "I have two more in the back room if you want to get those."

"Of course. The fetching will give me a break before I start painting."

"I can't wait to see this mighty guard dog when you're done," Rachel said, unpacking the wooden carvings neatly organized in the box.

Rachel

During downtime throughout the year, Nils carved several items for shoppers to buy for the Christmas holiday and stored them in the back room. He wanted to keep the months leading up to the holiday open for special orders. Each carving was a labor of love, and as Rachel unpacked them, she was reminded of the endless hours Nils spent hunched over the workbench each day.

Rachel placed carvings in the shop window to draw in customers.

"Have you made a plan on how you will design the gift carvings in the window?" Nils asked.

"I have a few things in mind, but I'm not sure which of your creations should be the centerpiece." Rachel picked up a wooden Advent calendar in the shape of a star.

The two-foot mahogany star was adorned with twenty-five numbered doors, each with a tiny wooden knob. Behind the doors, a small treasure filled each compartment. There were brightly colored tops, horses, and building blocks.

"This Advent calendar reminds me of the one you made for Stefan," she said with fond recollection. "He was so thrilled when you gave it to him."

Nils crossed the room and wrapped his arms around her. "He grinned from ear to ear."

She nodded. "Remember how he would get up so early each day, run first thing to the Advent calendar, and open the next door to see what was inside?"

"Yes. His squeals woke us up most mornings. The holidays were the only time in his life when he got out of bed that early." Nils chuckled as he put down the last box by the window.

"Putting in the new treasures each year was one of my favorite things about getting ready for Christmas when he was young," Rachel said.

"Every year it got harder to hide what I was making to fill the Advent calendar," Nils remembered. "I would catch Stefan snooping around my work area and had to wait till he was in bed at night just to work on them."

"He was such a rascal when he was a boy. But now Stefan is a strong, smart man, old enough to serve in the army." Rachel shook her head. "And to not come home after he's done. It's been two weeks since his conscription ended. Where could he be?"

"I don't know," Nils said, shaking his head too. "Maybe an opportunity arose that he couldn't pass up."

"But he didn't write? That's not like, Stefan. What if he is hurt or sick?" Rachel's voice trembled with worry.

"I agree it's not like him, and that concerns me as well, dear wife. So I sent a letter to his captain to see if he has any news. Hopefully, we will hear from Stefan or his captain soon."

Rachel began to feel a panic rise within her but tried to focus on the Scripture she had read that morning, Psalm 138:8. *The Lord will perfect that which concerns me,* she recited to herself. *Your mercy, O Lord, endures forever.* The words soaked into Rachel's being, and she felt a calm wash over her.

"Until we receive news of Stefan," she said, "we'll trust that the Creator is watching over him. I'm going to place the Advent calendar in the center, so Stefan will see it first thing when he returns."

Nils smiled. "That sounds perfect." He gave her another squeeze before returning to his workbench.

"I ran into Elia's nanny at the mercantile yesterday," Rachel said, dusting a row of Dala horses. "Duchess Sylvie was watching over Elia and encouraged Alma to take a break. Alma was buying some of Elia's favorite sweets to sit on her bedside table. I learned Alma blames herself for the girl being so sick."

"Why is that?" Nils asked.

"She had taken Elia out to play with her new hoop and stick in the afternoon. The sun was shining, so they bundled up and strolled with the hoop out into the lower grounds by Lake Hjälmaren. A rain shower started all of a sudden, and by the time Alma could get Elia back to the castle, they were both drenched and chilled."

"It is hard to predict the sudden weather changes here," Nils said, shaking his head. "Did you reassure Alma it wasn't her fault?"

“I did, but I don’t think it did much good. The castle staff did all the things they could—warm baths, lots of soup, hot water bottles in their beds. Still, both of them had a raging fever by the next morning. Alma recovered after a few days, but Elia has not.”

“The Creator knows how to comfort Alma,” Nils said. “Let’s ask Him to give her peace about this situation.”

“Wonderful idea,” Rachel said, wiping dust off one of the jewelry boxes and placing it on a stand in the window.

“Did Alma say how Elia is doing?” Nils asked.

“Not much change yet. Alma did say Elia sleeps with the characters you’ve made. She holds them close to her chest until she’s asleep, then Alma puts them back on her bedside table.”

“Well, that is something. I’m glad Elia’s enjoying them.”

“Do you have many more characters to make?” Rachel asked.

“I believe the Creator has quite the story to share,” Nils replied. “I will make all that He shows me.”

“I’m enjoying the story as well,” said Rachel. “The wee girl is in trouble, and I can’t wait to see how the woodcutter and his group of furry friends help her.”

Chapter 8

Tucker

I had just retrieved the fish from my hiding place when, out of nowhere, a blur flew at me. *What in the world?* I dropped the herring on the ground, snapped my head around, and bared my teeth.

A goose twice my size, wings stretched out, ran toward me. Beady eyes glaring, the goose cackled loudly, spraying me with spittle as it came close enough for me to notice the contrasting grey-and-white feathers covering its rotund body.

I did not move. The goose's display was ludicrous. Showing no fear, I growled. "How dare you come at me like that? Who do you think you are?"

"I am Grendela, and I'm someone who can make life very difficult for you. That's who *I* am. Who are *you* and what are you doing here?" The goose's voice was filled with a sense of authority, and her eyes bore into mine with a piercing gaze attempting dominance.

"That is none of your business." I moved to pick up my fish. The goose came at me again, slapping me with one of her wings.

"It is too my business, cur. You're trespassing. These woods around this fishing village belong to my flock and no one else."

"I am no cur, goose," I retorted. "I am an Irish terrier from the royal line of McGinty."

Grendela snickered. "La-di-da! McGinty or not, you're still trespassing."

She began to honk and charged closer. I darted away and put some distance between us, the sound of her honking echoing through the dense woods. I looked over my shoulder, and the man stirring the pot had turned to look our way.

"Keep your honking down, fool," I said in a low voice.

"Answer my question and I will," Grendela said.

"Okay, okay. I followed the wee lass here."

"Ah, the child." The goose retracted her wings. "What do you want with her?"

Ignoring her question, I said, "She seems to be in some kind of trouble."

Grendela turned to watch the girl hauling buckets. "She is a dear one and very kind to us animals. It breaks my heart to hear her sob every night as she lies out in the barn with us." Grendela's voice was filled with genuine concern. "I wish I could do more to help her, but I'm not sure what to do."

"Are you saying she sleeps in the barn?" I asked. "Why?"

"Don't know. The girl didn't come with us on the ship from Gävle in the spring. She showed up one day with *him*." Grendela tilted her head toward the large, stern man I'd witnessed speaking gruffly to the girl. "You could see the girl's fear of him in her eyes," Grendela continued. "He told her she needed to earn her keep and to put her belongings in the barn. Since then, she's worked from dawn to dark and collapses in the barn each night."

"A barn is no place for a human child," I said, shaking my head. "That is meant for our kind." Anger rose in my chest. "Something must be done."

"That girl has indeed had a hard time of it," Grendela said. "If you do anything to add to that sorrow, you will do it at your own peril." The goose honked loudly and hissed.

I growled. "Could you keep quiet? I'm not here to hurt the girl. My master has been leaving food out for her and wants to help. He sent me here to see what's going on."

"Oh," the goose said, speaking quieter. "In that case, how can I help?"

"You say the girl came with that man," I said, watching the gruff fisherman step back into the boat. "What's his name?"

"I've only heard the other fishermen call him Boss," Grendela replied.

"What does the girl call him?" I asked.

"She calls him uncle."

"Do you happen to know the girl's name?" I inquired.

"Runt is what they all call her," Grendela said woefully. "Never heard another name."

"Well, this is quite the predicament," I said. "I will head back to my master. He will know what to do."

"I don't see what he can do," she said, shaking her head. "The lass tried to run away once. Boss found her and told her there was no use in running away, because no one would ever want her."

"The scoundrel!" I sputtered angrily. "That's not true. My master cares about her. I need to go home and inform him. Watch over the girl while I'm gone. We're just a couple of miles to the north, at the first cabin outside Söderhamn. Come to us if you have any news to report." Before the goose could respond, I picked up the dirt-covered herring and ran for the cabin.

Due to my superior agility and sense of direction, the trip didn't take long. When I approached the cabin from the south, Anders was sitting in the chair outside, Clara in his lap.

"You're back," Clara said, licking her paws.

I dropped the fish at Anders's feet.

"What's this?" He picked up the fish. "A herring. So the girl is at a fishing village. I checked the ones to the north of Söderhamn. I didn't realize there was anyone in the southern one. Well done, Tucker!" He patted my head. "Can you take me there tomorrow?"

I yipped my agreement, and Anders walked into the house, humming softly.

"So you kept up with the girl?" Clara said. "I was sure you would lose her in the woods."

"Of course I kept up! The rough terrain drove me up and down like a fiddler's elbow, but I am trained for reconnaissance. I found out where she lives and much more. She gathers sticks on a sled in the woods. That's how she came to be near the cabin. She has a wretched uncle other fishermen call 'Boss.' He is very mean to her, works her day and night, and takes away her supper if she makes any kind of mistake. Plus, he makes her sleep in a barn!"

"What?!" Clara narrowed her eyes at me. "It's daytime. How did you find out she slept in a barn?"

"A bossy greylag goose named Grendela attacked me as I tried to return with the herring. She almost blew my cover, infernal goose! She had serious notions about me, but once she recognized I was of royal blood and trustworthy, she divulged the information about the uncle and the other details I needed."

"That poor girl," Clara said. "I don't know how Anders can help her if the man harming her is her kin."

"Anders will find a way," I reassured Clara, my confidence in my master unwavering. "I am certain of that."

Chapter 9

Nils

"It has come," Nils said, holding a tan envelope as he burst in the door. "A letter from Stefan's captain."

Nils closed the door quickly to avoid more snow blowing in. The weather had turned overnight, allowing for several inches of accumulation on the ground.

He could see Rachel shivering as the draft invaded their cozy kitchen. While Nils opened the envelope, she stirred a large bowl of currants, almonds, yeast, and spices.

"What does the captain say?" she asked, bracing herself with a hand on the counter.

Nils skimmed the letter. "That a previous letter he posted to us for Stefan must have gotten lost. He says Stefan and three other men went north with another member of their troop. This letter doesn't say why, just that Stefan went along to be helpful."

"That sounds like our Stefan." Rachel sighed. "If only the first letter would show up. Maybe then we would know what is going on."

"At least Stefan was well the last time the captain saw him. That is an answer to our prayers." Hugging her, Nils sniffed the fragrant kitchen air. "Your julbröd smells delicious. It's one of my favorite breads during the holiday season."

Rachel gave him a wry smile. "Have I baked a type of bread you don't like?"

"Not really because your baking has always been delicious. It's one of the perks of marrying you, my dear." He smiled back at her, then perused the ingredients on the table. "Are you making more?"

"Yes, I'm on my second batch. I made smaller, elf rolls with the first batch. I want to surprise the Modine children with them when I deliver their basket on Christmas Eve. It's always a joy to see their faces light up."

"You're going to frost them all, right?" Nils snuck a currant from the bowl.

Rachel slapped his hand. "I won't have enough to make a third batch if you keep eating those. Of course I'm frosting them. This batch is for the braided julbröd that will accompany the lutefisk I'm soaking for our holiday meal. Hopefully, Stefan will be home by Christmas to help eat all this."

"I'm sure he's doing everything he can to get home," Nils said. "There is some good news. I went to the castle this morning, to deliver my carving of Grendela the goose. I needed to stretch my legs and figured the castle staff would be busy getting ready for the upcoming holiday. Anyway—"

"Grendela is my favorite so far. What a protective goose she is!" Rachel chuckled, then turned somber. "Was there any news on Elia?"

"I was trying to tell you; that's the good news. Vincent met me at the door and invited me to the kitchen for morning fika with Brigitta. She said Elia drank a little cup of broth the duchess requested."

"Oh, that's a good sign." Rachel poured powdered sugar in a small bowl.

"Yes, and Vincent said Elia asks to hear the stories again each time she wakes. She tries to play with the animals but is still too weak to do so for long."

"The stories are helping, though. That is welcome news." Rachel's eyes shone with hope.

"The Creator always knows how to help." Nils pressed his palms together. "There are just seven days until Christmas. We pray she gets stronger and stronger each day."

"Amen," Rachel agreed.

Ting-a-ling-a-ling. Both Nils and Rachel turned toward the shop door at the ringing of the bell.

"I'll get it," he said, squeezing her hand. "You finish here. Maybe we can have some of your delectable treats with our supper tonight?"

She laughed. "Maybe."

After waiting on several customers, Nils combed through stacks of wood he'd gathered over the last few months. He always enjoyed his long walks in the forest, seeking fallen wood to dry for carving. Where others may have only seen trees, sticks, and branches, Nils saw creations ready to be revealed.

"Here it is," he said, pulling a large block of partially carved basswood from the stack. On finding the block during a fall outing in the south woods, he'd thought it perfect for carving a large Dala horse to surprise Stefan with this Christmas. Imagining the figure emerging from the wood reminded Nils of the first Dala horse he had given Stefan.

"Papa, is it mine?" Stefan's mouth had hung open as he eyed the horse in the box.

"Yes, just for you," Nils had told him.

Nils had noticed Stefan studying the Dala horses in the shop's window several times. Even though Stefan was just four years old, Nils had spent many of Rachel's candles to carve the little red-and-yellow horse late at night.

"Such pretty colors, Papa!" Stefan had exclaimed.

Nils smiled to himself now. It seemed such a short time ago when his son was that young.

This year, Nils had decided to make a much larger version from the forty-five-by-sixty centimeter block of basswood. He would paint the horse the colors of the Swedish flag to commemorate Stefan's first military service.

Nils placed the block on the table and rubbed his hand over the head he'd carved before the holiday season. He'd worked with the flow of the grain to carve the horse's nose in perfect symmetry on both sides. Humming "Silent Night," the wood-carver applied light pressure with his flat-edged chisel and shaved tiny slivers of wood off the block, rounding the edges of the body to form the correct thickness. He patiently found the form of the legs and hindquarters.

On completion of each section, he took time to clean the sawdust off his workbench and wait for the Creator to give insight on the piece.

Slowly, Nils carved down one of the back legs, going just to the top of the hoof. Whittling legs was always saved for last, to ensure he didn't break one off while working on other parts of the piece. Nils's father had warned that sculpting all the way down to the bottom of the leg could cause the last few layers of wood to snap off. So Nils chiseled down just to the top of each hoof and then changed directions, carving upward on the hooves to round each one.

He made a small valley between one of the horse's legs and the belly, the wood-carver's chisel deftly removing layers of wood. Then he switched to a small V-cut tool that defined the belly and the outline of the leg.

His hands almost moved like a painter's, in a symphony of pressure and strokes. As he worked the figure, he remembered a long-ago conversation he'd had with Vincent about Stefan.

"Nils, your Stefan certainly looks like you," Vincent had said. "You must be so proud."

"I am blessed with this boy that the Creator has given us. However, he has a strong desire for adventure and trying new things, like my older brother."

"I can see that in him. From the upstairs window in the castle, I see Stefan roaming in the trees with his wooden sword most afternoons." Vincent chuckled.

He hardly slept the night before he left for his conscription. I guess we really shouldn't be surprised that our son has taken off with one of his fellow soldiers, Nils thought now, studying Rachel as she dusted carvings in the shop window. *I'm sure he will have quite the tale to tell us when he returns.*

Christmas would be very quiet this year if Stefan didn't make it home. The young man had such a contagious belly laugh that he couldn't help but fill the house with merriment.

Nils gazed upward. "Dear Lord, keep our Stefan safe. Bring him home to us for Christmas." The wood-carver paused. "But if he can't be home, surround him with people who will celebrate the birth of the Christ Child as it should be. Amen."

Chapter 10

Siv

"There's no better keeper in all the north country than yours, Siv," a neighbor horse called to me as I trod past. "I've been working hard for my keeper, hauling trees and clearing fields, and he doesn't look after me like Anders does you."

"Yeah," said another neighbor. "I wish I would have put on more of show when Anders came to our farm in search of a horse."

I already knew that most North Swedish draft horses didn't have a keeper like mine. Anders looked like all keepers in the north country—tall, light brown hair, and blue-eyed. But that was where his similarities ended. Anders knew that no horse was meant to be owned. We're not like goats who give milk for drinking or chickens who lay eggs for eating. We work alongside the keeper as a partner of sorts, and if there is rhythm between the horse and his counterpart, the teamwork makes the workload lighter.

After hauling several logs to the cabin, I shook my long mane from my eyes and joined Tucker McGinty in watching Anders prop a log between two smaller stumps. While the woodsman sawed the log, his thick arms moved back and forth, and the rasping of his saw resounded in the clearing. The log landed in two pieces on the blanket of sawdust covering the ground.

Anders repeated the process with the other logs, then began stacking the cut wood in the large pile near the cabin. "Almost done here, Siv. Then we'll see what Tucker found out about the hungry girl who comes by the cabin."

A sudden cool gale of a breeze whipped around us as Anders cinched my saddle. He grabbed his brown woolen coat and stocking hat from the wood pile before stroking my mane. "We best get moving. Come on, Tucker. Show me where the hungry girl lives, and let's see if we can help her."

Tucker paraded in front of us, trotting like he was in a military parade. Many of the farm's animals often snickered at him, especially the cat. But I gave the sentinel his due. He, too, was a worker alongside our keeper, protecting the farm.

We wound along a barely visible path, veering around bushes and fording a small stream. It was some time before we approached a clearing.

"Whoa, Siv. Let's stop here so I can see what's going on." Anders dismounted and stood behind a tree.

I stretched my neck around the tree and saw several boats on the water, men inside them pulling on large nets. More men on shore gutted fish and threw the innards into buckets.

"There she is," Anders said as a girl came around the corner of a fishing shanty with an empty bucket.

"Get a move on, runt," a humpbacked man yelled at her. "The buckets are almost full. Get them emptied into the barrel. Take two of them instead of just one."

The girl dropped the empty bucket and struggled to pick up two full ones.

"Put your back into it," said the man. "They aren't that heavy."

The girl shuffled her feet, carrying the load of fish innards and heads. Her woolen coat had no buttons and flapped open in the wind. Her hands and face were red and chapped, as she didn't have fur on her face like Anders and me.

"The poor child," Anders said. "It is worse than I thought. That wee girl can't do all of that work."

Tucker bared his teeth suddenly, and I turned toward movement in the bushes. I saw a flash of grey and white, then felt a weight on my back. I shook furiously to dislodge whatever sat on me. Tucker growled as a goose plopped to the ground next to us.

"It's me, you fool dog," the goose said. "Who is this beast with you?"

"Hush up!" Tucker said in a furious whisper. "My master's horse has come with us to look over the girl's situation, and we don't need to be spotted. Siv, this goose, Grendela, lives with the girl in the barn and has a problem with being quiet."

Tucker rejoined Anders at watching the fishing village. Grendela turned her head to stare at me with one of her beady black eyes, which made me chuckle.

"Mighty rude introduction there, goose," I said, smirking. "Jumping on someone's back without permission is just not done."

"Sorry about that. I get a little jumpy when I see a new critter. I figure it's better to show your strength right out of the gate, let someone know who is boss. It's my job to roam these woods and keep out troublemakers like him." She looked at Tucker.

"Well, I am not a troublemaker. I'm here with my keeper." I nodded toward Anders.

Grendela looked Anders up and down. "Do you think the cur is right that this Anders can help the girl?"

Tucker turned around with a huff. "Of course he can! We just need silence to be able to figure out a plan, so shush up."

"Don't you be rude to me, mutt," Grendela said.

While the goose and dog bickered, a boat had come to shore. I snorted, and we all watched a large man get out of the boat and walk to the humpbacked man.

"That large man is the one they call Boss," Tucker said. "He's the girl's uncle."

"Where's the girl?" Boss asked.

"Emptying buckets," said the hunchbacked man.

The girl came limping around the corner, the two buckets she carried now empty, tears in her downcast eyes.

"Now what've you done?" Boss bellowed.

Not looking up, she said, "I fell, Uncle. I tried to empty the buckets, but I slipped in the mud."

"Did you clean it up?" he asked sternly.

"Yes," she said, a sob escaping from her lips.

"There'll be no crying," the girl's uncle said. "You'll earn your keep here. Do you hear me? I was doing this job when I was your age. You just need to toughen up."

"Yes, sir." The girl walked to the line of full pails. Glancing toward the woods, she saw my keeper, and a wave of fright washed over her face. I had not seen that type of fear for a long time, not since my keeper had been surprised by a Eurasian wolf while we were in the woods one day.

Anders put his index finger to his lips. The girl looked away, picked up two more buckets, and struggled to carry them to the barrel, not looking behind her.

"This is not good," Anders said. "I've seen enough. I need to pray about what to do. That man being her uncle makes this more difficult, but nothing is impossible when you know the Father."

He grabbed my reins and mounted my back.

I turned my head. "Goose, can you keep an eye on the girl for us? I'm sure we will be back soon."

"I'd be delighted," Grendela said before turning to Tucker. "Dog, you could take some lessons from Siv on how to be polite." Tucker only growled as the goose sauntered off.

Following my keeper's tug on the reins, I plodded away from the clearing, over the brook, through the large grove of trees, and back to our cabin. Anders spoke not a word on the way home.

Dappled sunlight came through the tree branches around the cabin. Anders dismounted and sat down on the wooden chair, closing his eyes.

"Father," he said, "You know what this poor girl is going through."

Tucker and I looked at each other. Anders was doing it again. Talking to his Father, though there was no one was around.

"No child should be working that hard," he said. "You were there for me when I was a boy, a hurting orphan no one loved. I believe You have sent this girl to us for a reason. I'm sure there is something You want me to do, but I don't know what that is. Heavenly Father, please show me how to help her."

After shaking the trip's snow off my mane, I stood quietly. I didn't understand what my keeper was doing, but whenever Anders spoke like that, good things began to happen.

Chapter 11

Nils

"Are you making more Advent stars?" Nils asked Rachel, noticing red paper, string, and glue pots covering the kitchen table. He stepped to the stove and filled his cup with steaming brown coffee.

"I will be. When I walked by the Modines' home yesterday, I noticed they didn't have any decorations in their window and asked Fionda if I could visit this morning." Rachel snugged the supplies into an already overflowing basket. "I'm hoping to give Fionda a break by crafting Advent stars with the children. Then they can place them in the windows."

"What a wonderful and thoughtful idea," Nils replied, his smile widening as he admired Rachel's initiative.

"Will you need to deliver to the castle this morning?" she asked, adding some milk to her coffee.

"Not today. But I'm working on a new carving for Elia."

"And what character is next in the story?" Rachel asked as she sat down at the table, swishing her coffee with a spoon.

"A horse has joined the story. Siv is a sturdy, dependable, mild-tempered North Swedish horse with a deep appreciation for his keeper. I'm trying to capture his loyalty and strength in my carving."

"He sounds delightful. When I was growing up, my family had a North Swedish mare. They are the best for farming." Rachel eyed Nils thoughtfully as she took a sip of her coffee. "You've had lots of experience making Dala horses over the years, so I am looking forward to seeing Siv when you're done."

A comfortable silence fell over them. The wood-carver watched his wife have a far-off look. Soon, the lines between her eyes began to crinkle. He knew this meant she was thinking of Stefan again. He picked up her hand and held it in his as she looked at him with an anxious face.

"What's on your mind?" Nils asked.

"There's a wet chill in the air. More snow is coming." Heavy concern tinged her voice. "Even if Stefan is headed this way, what if he gets caught in the storm?"

Nils mustered a voice of reassurance. "Maybe Stefan's letter will arrive today and we will know something more about his plans. As we wait, we will help others—the Modines and Elia. In turn, the Creator will take care of our Stefan wherever he is."

Rachel sighed and got up from the table. "You're right. I will bake another batch of cookies and spend the afternoon with the Modine children."

The shop doorbell jingled. Nils rose and kissed Rachel on the cheek. "Back to it for me as well."

Rachel

Under a light fall of snowflakes, delicate and cold, Rachel made her way across the street, then walked four blocks to a group of smaller homes along the bank of Lake Hjälmaren. She rapped on a white door with a small black number six painted on it. She had barely finished knocking when the door swung open and the youngest Modine boy smiled up at her. Fredrik was five years old, with a rosy face, blue eyes, and almost white hair.

"Come in, Frau Kindberg," he said, his voice filled with fondness. "We've been waiting for you."

A snicker erupted from behind the door.

"We?" Rachel asked Frederik teasingly. "Who could be behind the door?"

A burst of giggles broke out, then a three-year-old girl with plaited blond hair, grey-blue eyes, and a dress checked with red and white peeked around the corner of the door.

"Ina!" Rachel said, smiling. "I would have never guessed you were behind there."

Fionda came into the kitchen doorway, wiping flour off her apron, her face flushed. "Good morning, Rachel. It's snowing again, I see."

"Good morning, Fionda. Yes, it appears we'll have a snowy Christmas." Rachel held the basket she carried out to Fionda. "I brought you a few things to ease your holidays."

Fionda took the basket and looked into it. "Oh, Rachel! So many wonderful things, dear friend. May the Creator bless you for your kindness."

Rachel squeezed Fionda's hand. "How is Charles getting along?"

"He is able to get up and around more but still spends most of his days resting."

"I'm glad to hear he's improving." Rachel pointed into the basket. "I brought some supplies to craft Advent stars with the children, if that's okay with you."

A clamor of feet running down the stairs brought ten-year-old fraternal twins Jarl and Janna into the room. Fionda halted their charge by setting one hand on Jarl's dark blond head and the other on Janna's strawberry-blond one.

"Please, Mama," the twins pled in unison, "can we make Advent stars with Frau Kindberg?" Jarl's dark blue eyes and Janna's cornflower-blue ones shone with anticipation.

"Good children do not raise such a racket while their papa is trying to rest," Fionda scolded.

"Sorry, Mama," they said, lowering their voices.

"You can craft with Frau Kindberg here in the sitting room, if you can be quieter." Fionda winked at Rachel.

"We promise to be quieter," they said as all the children gathered around a low table.

"I will leave you to it, then," Fionda said. "I have some things to finish in the kitchen."

Rachel began placing supplies on the table—strips of red paper, strings for hanging the stars, and two glue pots. She placed several paper strips and a piece of string at four places around the table.

"Frau Kindberg, what is Herr Kindberg working on today?" Jarl asked.

"He's carving a horse named Siv, for a little girl who has been very sick."

"Is it for Elia?" Janna asked.

"It is." Rachel opened the tubs of glue.

"She has been sick a long time," Jarl said. "Janna and I were sick, but we are much better now."

"It's good that you are both better," Rachel said, adding a place with supplies at the head of the table for herself. "We are all praying Elia, too, will be well soon. Sit down children, each of you at one of the four spots, and I will help you in making the Advent stars."

"Could I make an Advent star for Elia?" Janna asked.

The suggestion touched Rachel. "What a superb idea!"

"I want to make one for her too," Jarl said.

"So do I," Fredrick said, turning to Ina. "Do you want to make one?"

"Me too, please," Ina said with a bit of a lisp.

"Well, we better get started if we are making stars for you and Elia," Rachel said, laughing. "It's a good thing I brought plenty of supplies. Jarl and Janna, can you count to twelve?"

"Yes," they replied in unison.

"Please count out twelve of these strips total for each of us," Rachel instructed. "Who can tell me why we make Advent stars?"

"To remind us of the three wise men following the Christmas star," Jarl said. "Mother just read us that story last night."

"And to decorate our windows with candles and stars," Janna added as she laid paper strips by Rachel's seat, "to remind others of the Christ Child that came."

"Yes, very good," Rachel said, pleased. "Does everyone have twelve strips?"

All the children nodded.

"We will have to share the pots of glue. Each of you take two of your strips, like this." Rachel held two strips up and waited. "Fold them in half, then glue one on top of the other to make a cross."

"The cross is part of the Christ Child's story too," Janna said.

“Yes, it is,” Rachel agreed, helping Fredrick with the glue. “So it’s fitting that our Advent stars start with a cross. Who knows how to weave?”

Four hands shot up, and Rachel grinned. “Let’s weave some beautiful stars, some to put up in your window tonight and some to give to Elia. We have just four more days till Christmas Eve.”

Rachel demonstrated weaving the strips into a star shape, then watched as the children began weaving their own. How she hoped Elia would be well enough to enjoy the stars made for her.

Chapter 12

Clara

While I was catnapping in a bit of afternoon sunshine, I heard my woodsman say, "Father, please help the hungry girl know that she can come here for food. Show me how to help her out of the situation she's in. I know You love her and will take care of her as You have taken care of me." Many times throughout the last few weeks, Anders had stopped whatever he was doing and talked this way.

Tucker walked up, blocking the sun I was enjoying. "I have searched high and low and do not see this Father the master continues to speak to."

"I don't see him either," I said, moving out of the dog's shadow. "But there are many human behaviors I don't understand."

Anders walked out of the cabin, the aroma of wood smoke and a stew simmering on the fire wafting out the door with him. He picked up several milk pails and headed to the barn.

Tucker trotted behind, glancing back over his shoulder. "I'll follow and let you know if I see the Father he keeps talking to."

They hadn't been gone long when I saw familiar red locks appear in the bushes. Slowly, the girl stepped out of hiding and walked to the tin Anders had placed on the chair. She looked inside but did not take the food. Instead, she slid the tin back and sat on the edge of the chair.

I sauntered over and began rubbing against her legs as a warm welcome. The girl picked me up, stroking my fur. Her hands were chapped and rough, but I didn't mind. She hugged me close, and I could see her hair was disheveled and dirty, her cheeks rosy from the cold.

"You are such a pretty kitty," the girl said. Out of one eye, I spotted Tucker approaching and gave him a sharp look. Ears up and tail erect, he appeared about to bark. Then he seemed to think twice about it and lay down by the corner of the cabin, watching.

When Anders also appeared at the corner, the girl was scratching behind my ears. He paused and waited where he stood until she looked up. I was surprised she didn't bolt away.

Anders walked up to us slowly. "Good morning. It's been quite a while since you were here last."

“I couldn’t get away,” the girl said. “May I have some of the food in the tin?”

“Of course,” my woodsman answered with a reassuring tone. “There’s bread and soft cheese here for you. My wife makes the best cheese in the entire county.”

“You have a wife?” the girl asked, looking puzzled.

Anders laughed and leaned against the doorway to the cabin. “Yes. Her name is Maja. She’s been away helping her sister who's been ill. Maja is coming home on the train, today. I’ve written to her and she’s eager to get home and meet you.”

The girl’s eyebrows shot up. “She wants to meet *me*?”

He nodded.

The girl sniffed the cheese, then took a nibble. “Delicious!” she exclaimed, her mouth already full from taking a larger bite. After chewing and swallowing yet another bite, she cocked her head to one side and looked at Anders. “Why did you come to the fishing village the other day?”

“I wondered where you lived. Have you been at the fishing village long?”

“Not long. I used to live in Stockholm. What’s your name?”

“Goodness!” Anders cried. “I should’ve introduced myself long ago. My name is Anders Dahl, and the cat sitting on your lap is Clara.”

“I am Leena,” she said, as Tucker strode over. “Leena Selberg.”

“Our dog is Tucker McGinty,” Anders said.

The dog struck a ridiculous rigid pose, which I am sure he thought showed authority, but it only made my woodsman and Leena break into giggling. I squinted my eyes at them to show I was laughing too.

"Tucker is a wonderful guard dog," Anders said, regaining his composure. "How old are you, Leena? I'm guessing about nine or ten."

"Ten. I'd just had my birthday before—" Leena's eyes welled with sudden tears. "Before my parents died."

"I'm so sorry," my woodsman told her. "I lost my parents too, when I was twelve. I was sent to live in an orphanage."

"Oh. I have to live with my uncle." Leena sighed deeply, then chewed and swallowed a bite of bread. "What was it like living in an orphanage? Did you sleep in a bed?"

"I slept in a room with seven other boys. We each had our own bed."

"I used to have my own bed too and lots of food." Leena took a drink from the cup. "How long were you there?"

"Two years. One day several of us were told to dress in our Sunday clothes and gather in the main hall. We soon found out they were holding a barnauktion."

"A what?"

"A barnauktion," Anders repeated. "Several couples milled about the hall, talking with each of us. After some time, the couples sat down and the director called us up one by one and the bidding began."

"They sold you?" the girl cried.

"In a way," he said. "It was hard to understand at first. The authorities auctioned us off to the families to help reduce the cost of our care. A farming couple took me on, and I worked alongside the farmer in the fields most days. It was long days, but the couple educated me and introduced me to a loving Father."

Leena's shoulders drooped. "It is hard being alone."

"I found out I was never truly alone," Anders said. "My Father was and is always with me."

The girl and Tucker looked at him curiously.

"I eventually grew up and moved to Söderhamn where I met Maja." Anders stepped up to the cabin door. "Let me get you more food." He returned and handed Leena another piece of bread and a cup of milk.

She put the bread in her pocket, drank the milk, and gave the cup to Anders. After gently setting me on the ground, she trudged toward the forest. "I best get back before I get in trouble. I'm supposed to be collecting wood." She trudged toward the bushes, retrieving a sled half full of branches.

"Would you like me to help you fill this sled?" my woodsman asked. "And pull it back to the fishing village?"

"If you want to," Leena said. "But you can't let my uncle see you. He won't be happy I had help from anyone."

"I'll stay out of sight," Anders reassured her. He grabbed the rope on the sled.

Tucker McGinty began to follow along, but Anders turned around.

"No, boy," he directed in a low tone. "Stay here this time and give Maja a warm welcome home." My woodsman's eyes brightened. "I've heard from my Father and have much to talk over with her."

Anders and Leena walked out of sight, chatting amiably.

"Humph!" Tucker said to himself. "How are they going to know where to go without me?"

I snickered. "I think the girl has made that trip many times. Did you hear Anders say he heard from his Father? And that bit about his Father always being with him? Strange. We've had no visitors. And I have no idea how he thinks he can help that girl."

"Maybe his Father wrote to him," Tucker suggested. "I know my master will determine how to help the girl." He sauntered off to the barn.

That could be, I thought as I curled up in another sunny spot to catch forty winks. If I wanted to hear all that Anders meant to share with Maja, I'd need to resist the urge to nap in front of tonight's fire.

Chapter 13

Nils

Nils closed his eyes and let his mind fill again with the image of Anders that had greeted him on waking that morning. The wood-carver had swiftly sketched the woodcutter's warm, friendly face on kraft paper he kept by his bedside. Opening his eyes, he gazed from the sketch in his hand to the stack of wood before him. He chose a piece of mahogany wood, its rich, reddish-brown hue a perfect match for the carving he envisioned.

His hands explored the wood, tracing the grain and meticulously planning the carving. He had decided to depict Anders in work attire, as if about to embark on a day of tree felling. The wood-carver marked the block at the midpoint, denoting the waist. On the upper half, he sketched three equal sections for the head, shoulders, and lower torso, preparing for the character to come to life.

Pulling out his favorite chisel, Nils applied steady pressure, removing layer upon layer of wood, cutting upward and downward to make the stop cuts that designated each distinct area.

Rachel breezed into the shop with a tray.

"Do you have a moment for fika? I've prepared a tray of spitzbuben just for you." Her eyes fell on the worktable, now covered with curls of mahogany. "You've been busy, I see. What animal are you carving?"

"Not an animal this time, but the woodcutter. I'm just finishing this arm." After a few cuts, he joined Rachel at the table. "I forgot to ask how crafting with the Modine children went yesterday."

"It went very well. In fact, I'm meeting with the children at their home again today."

"The crafting must have been a great success if you're going again," Nils said. "Or have the children requested more of your delicious cookies?"

Rachel laughed. "They decided to make Advent stars for Elia. Since Fionda has her hands full with Charles and extra sewing work, I told her I would take the children to deliver the stars to the castle today."

"Excellent. I'm sure it will cheer not only Elia but the entire castle to know others are thinking of her."

"I agree." Rachel glanced at the Dala horse Nils had started for Stefan. "And crafting and gifting keep my thoughts pleasant as well."

Rachel

When she and Nils had finished fika, Rachel returned the tray to the kitchen. She rinsed out the cups and laid them on a towel to dry before putting on her coat and scarf. Bracing for the cold, she was pleasantly surprised to find the wind had died down and only a few flakes of snow were falling.

She made her way across the street and down the blocks to the Modine home, where she barely knocked before the door swung open. Four smiling faces greeted her.

Rachel laughed. "Are we all ready to go to the castle?" The children's excitement bubbled from them like water from a pot about to boil over.

"We have everything ready," Janna said, patting a basket she carried on her arm.

"We made cards for Elia last night," Fredrik told Rachel, his eyes shining with pride. "Mine has a Christmas tree on the front."

"I drew cookies on mine," Ina said, her voice squeaking.

"Mine has a horse and sleigh," Jarl added as Fionda appeared behind him.

"Your beautiful decorations and cards are sure to make Elia feel special," Rachel said, smiling at each of the children and then at Fionda. "While we're out, Fionda, are there any errands we can do for you?"

"That is very kind," Fionda said, helping Ina pull on her mittens and then patting Frederik on the head. "But I can think of nothing. You children mind Frau Kindberg and be on your best behavior. Jarl and Janna, hold hands with Frederik and Ina as you walk."

Over the children's heads, Fionda mouthed a thank-you to Rachel, who nodded and clapped her hands. "Let's go, children. We have gifts to deliver!"

The five of them left the Modines' house and made their way along the wooden sidewalks, over the drawbridge, and onto the small islet that housed the castle in the middle of the Svartån River. The air was crisp, and the sound of their footsteps echoed off the weathered thirty-foot walls encasing the castle, a plastered cannon tower on each corner.

"We have never been inside the castle," Jarl said as they approached the front door. "We've just counted the windows on the front of the castle from the other side of the river."

"There are thirty-eight windows," Janna told Rachel.

"Thirty-nine." Jarl said. "Don't forget the round one at the very top."

"And that is only one side," Rachel commented, knocking on the door.

"Do you think we will get to see Elia?" Frederik asked as they waited.

"I don't think so," Rachel told him. "She is most likely resting in her room."

The front door opened, and Vincent, looked from Rachel to the children and back. "Good day! What brings your troop to the castle this wintry afternoon?"

"We brought Advent stars we made for Elia," Janna said.

"And cards," Frederik added.

"What a treat!" Vincent exclaimed with a wide grin. "Please come in."

Rachel and the children stepped into a large vestibule lined with life-sized statues and alabaster busts resting on marble stands, each depicting a Swedish monarch.

"I will take your coats and then show you to the Yellow Room, where the Duchess is spending the afternoon." Somehow, Vincent slung all their coats, scarves, and hats over one arm and directed them with a sweep of the other. "Right this way."

He led them into a large room with cream-colored walls, a red Persian rug, and seats upholstered in golden yellow damask fabric. Along the walls, a golden decorative border featuring a Greek key motif framed large oil paintings of family members and scenery. The duchess was seated in front of a fireplace, reading a book.

"Frau Kindberg and the Modine children to see you, ma'am," Vincent announced.

"What a treat on this dreary afternoon," the duchess said, putting down her book. "What has brought you out in this weather?"

"The children have brought some things for Elia," Rachel said, nodding to Janna.

"We made Advent stars for her room," Janna said, pulling several stars out of the basket she carried.

"And we made cards," Jarl said.

"We want her to feel better," Frederik chimed in. "So she can have Christmas."

"How thoughtful!" Duchess Sylvie exclaimed. "I can't wait for Elia to see all you have brought her,"

"Is she feeling any better?" Fredrick asked.

"Somewhat. But still not well enough to be out bed." Duchess Sylvie sighed, and the children's faces filled with concern. "But I am sure she will be back to her old self soon," the duchess assured them. "Since you have come all this way, how about some hot cocoa and cookies?"

Frederik and Ina clapped happily. Janna gave them a sharp look, and both children quieted.

"The sound of happy children warms me," Duchess Sylvie said, turning to Vincent. "Will you ask Brigitta for some cocoa and cookies for our guests?"

"Of course, m'lady," he said before exiting the room.

After Rachel returned the children to their home later that afternoon, she couldn't wait to tell Nils all about their excursion.

"It sounds like a huge success," Nils remarked. "Not only delivering the gifts for Elia, but it sounds like you raised the spirits of the duchess as well."

Rachel chuckled. "The children definitely did that. Duchess Sylvie was very somber when we arrived but smiling when we left. You were right. It is important for us to continue to help others even when we have concerns of our own."

Nils opened his arms, and Rachel slipped into them, resting her ear against his chest and listening to the rumble of his reassuring voice. "I know you still worry. Our concerns for Stefan are heard by the Creator, so now we have only to wait for His answer."

Chapter 14

Clara

Once Maja returned home, Leena came by more often. Maja would invite her into the cabin, where Leena sat in front of the fire to get warm. She held me in her lap, stroking my fur, and began to open up more and more about growing up in Stockholm.

Anders mostly sipped coffee quietly while listening to Leena's stories. After, he'd tell Maja he needed to talk with his Father, then go off for walks in the woods without Siv or the wagon.

"We lived behind the forge in a warm home," Leena told Maja and Anders one day. "My pa was very busy with his work, so I helped my mother when I wasn't in school." Tears filled the girl's eyes. "I miss them so much."

“I’m sure you do,” Maja said, reaching out for Leena’s hand.

“I used to have a kitty.” Leena sniffled. “But I had to give her to the neighbors in Stockholm. Uncle said it was enough to take care of me—he wasn’t feedin’ no cat.”

Eyes wide, Maja shook her head. “I’m so sorry, Leena. We’re happy to share Clara with you.”

Anders sat down his coffee and leaned toward Leena and myself. “We would be happy to share even more than that if you’d like. But we need to know if you’re interested in staying with us instead of at the fishing village?” My woodsman’s voice was filled with compassion.

Leena shrugged. “One barn is the same as any other,” she said, patting my head.

“Not in our barn, Leena,” Anders explained. “You would live with us in the cabin.”

“I would stay in the cabin with you?” Leena asked uncertainly.

“No child should be living in a barn,” Maja said. “Winter has arrived, and you should be in a home with a warm fire and good food.”

“I don’t see how that could ever happen,” Leena said sorrowfully. “Uncle will never allow it. When the officials told him he had to take me, he was very angry until he learned he’d receive money if he provided for me until I was of age. He signed papers but later told me I would have to earn my keep—after all, I wasn't his child, just a burden." More tears flowed down Leena's face.

"It may be difficult to convince your uncle," Anders said. "But I talked with my Father, and He gave me a plan."

Leena began to sob. "I miss my father."

Maja enveloped the crying girl in her arms. "Oh, poor child! Of course you miss him."

Anders knelt beside them and gave Leena his handkerchief. "Leena, you are not alone. How about I share my Father with you? Would you like that?"

"I thought you were an orphan like me," she said, wiping her tears.

"I am. But I have a new Father that has always helped me. I will tell you more about Him soon."

Maja's eyes moistened and she excused herself to prepare food.

"I better get back." Leena put me down. "I need to gather more wood for the fire. I don't want to get in trouble again."

"I'll help you," said Anders. I've gathered some sticks for you in a pile behind the barn. Tomorrow, I will work things out with your uncle." Anders walked over to Maja, speaking quietly. "I will be back to help you with chores. But first I'll help Leena get back to the fishing village."

"Good idea," Maja said as she wrapped a large wedge of cheese and a hunk of bread in a piece of cloth.

"I still don't think talking to uncle will make any difference," Leena said, handing Anders his handkerchief.

"Let us worry about that," Maja said, giving Leena the bundle of food and brushing hair away from the girl's eyes. "Go now with Anders, so he can fill your sled for you."

"Thank you," Leena said. She walked to the cabin door, then turned around, rushed to Maja, and hugged her fiercely.

Pip

The day was warm for late autumn, so I flew to the generous woodsman's cabin, to see if he had more seeds I could cache before winter. I lit atop the cabin roof and was surprised to see a woman come out the door. Wooden shoes protected her feet, and she wore a long-sleeved, cream-colored shirt.

She carried a tub of water and stooped to empty it at the side of the cabin. As she stood back up, I could see her smiling face. A light-blue scarf covered her head, and her skirt was made of brown wool.

The woman wiped her hands on her blue-and-white-striped apron as the woodsman came around the corner. "Maja, do you know where I laid the stocking hat you knitted me? There is a chill in the air, and I want to wear it on the journey."

"It's on the table, Anders," she said with a chuckle. "Where you left it after breakfast. Would you like another cup of coffee to warm you before you go?"

"No thanks. I have just finished chores and loading the sled, so I am ready to leave," Anders embraced Maja in a hug. "Leena needs our help. A young girl needs to be living in a home, not a barn."

"That poor child," Maja said, following him to the dooryard. "How could anyone be so cruel?" Her voice was full of empathy.

Anders shook his head. "I don't know, but the Father has given me an idea, and I hope to relieve some of her suffering." I could see he was determined.

"My prayers go with you," Maja said before kissing her woodsman on the cheek.

He took hold of his horse's reins and headed off through the bushes.

"Well, Clara," Maja said to a tabby cat sleeping under the chair, "we may have a guest staying with us for a while.

Yikes! Wrapped up in studying the new woman at the cabin, I hadn't even seen the cat. I flitted up to the roof, making more distance between me and the yellow monster.

"I better prepare a place for her and make a warm soup and bread for lunch," Maja said, walking into the cabin.

Had Anders and Maja been talking about the hungry red-haired girl who visited when I was here last? I decided to follow the woodsman and see for myself. He moved slowly, leading the horse down a winding path, a heavy load of split wood on the wagon.

Once the pair reached the stream, Anders turned to the horse. "We'll cross the stream here, Siv. Where the water is lowest."

Siv neighed and followed Anders into the stream. I felt lucky I didn't have to walk into that cold water. My feathers, although water-resistant, are not impervious to the cold. With the chill in the air that morning, the water had to be frigid.

After crossing the stream, it didn't take long before we arrived at the edge of a clearing. There was a strong odor in the frosty breeze, and I could hear people talking. From a high branch of a tree, I saw a fishing village. Could the girl be there?

Anders stayed out of sight behind some trees and stood still for several minutes, bowing his head and muttering some words I could not hear. Then I saw her, the red-haired girl, hauling an armful of sticks toward a fire. I let out a long trill of my most beautiful song, as I was so happy to see her again.

She looked toward the woods and saw Anders behind the tree. The same fear I'd seen before washed over her face, then she dropped her eyes and quickly walked to the fire with her load. My heart sank. What was the girl afraid of?

Chapter 15

Rachel

A knocking sound woke Rachel. She opened her eyes to darkness, turned over, and listened. *Bang-bang*. The dressmaker's sign next door made that noise when gale winds came off the lake.

Rachel sighed. A strong winter wind would undoubtedly bring a blizzard. Not good traveling weather. Gently throwing back the bedcovers, she went to the room's small fireplace, used the poker to stir the coals, and added a few more logs.

She turned to gaze at Nils, sleeping soundly. He had worked late in the shop, finishing the carving of Anders. She couldn't wait to see it. It always amazed her how her husband's hands, large enough to envelop hers, could chisel a piece of wood into a creation of such fine detail.

After dressing, she stirred up the fire in the shop as well, before taking a peek at the carving. The woodcutter's face smiled back at her. She gasped. How could a piece of wood show such love and compassion?

Nils's arms wrapped around her. "What do you think?" he whispered in her ear.

"I don't think I've ever seen a wooden figure show such sentiment," she said, her voice filled with admiration for her husband's talent.

"I felt the Creator helping me. It's important for Elia to see love in Anders's face. He is a reminder of the love that the Creator has for us."

Rachel marveled. "His expression captures that completely." A gust of wind rattled the windows. "Oh dear! The snow will come soon, and we don't have a Christmas tree yet. Have you time to go with me to find one?"

"Since I have more work to finish on Elia's gift and Stefan's, I asked the delivery boy who dropped off your lingonberry boughs yesterday if he could procure us a tree." From his workbench, Nils lifted a small chestnut box engraved with holly. "The boy and I struck a bargain with this box for his mother. He'll deliver the tree tomorrow morning."

"Nicely done, husband," Rachel said, smiling. "I better start breakfast and make our lingonberry wreath before the shop opens. I just hope the snow holds off until after Christmas."

Nils looked out the window. "I'm sorry to say the sky has darkened and the snow is already beginning to fall."

Rachel straightened her shoulders. "Well, I'm going to prepare the house for Christmas nonetheless and still believe Stefan will make it."

Nils smiled and added another log to the fire, filling the shop with warmth before he opened it for the day. Soon, they sat down to porridge and crisp macka bread, smothered in a fig spread and topped with hard cheese. Nils started his second cup of coffee since tidying his worktable.

"Will you deliver your Anders carving today?" Rachel asked, adding extra cheese to her macka. "Or is Vincent coming to retrieve it?"

"Someone from the castle will come for it today, though Vincent told me he won't be available. The castle is preparing to receive invited guests. With the storm coming in, I imagine they will arrive sooner than originally expected."

"I cannot imagine how busy the castle servants will be," Rachel said. "Since you're done with Anders, what character will you work on today?"

"I've been seeking the Creator on that this morning. I believe it will be the wee girl. Leena."

"That will certainly be of interest to Elia," Rachel said. "The girl is about her age."

"It will be a challenge to capture the sadness of what Leena is going through." Nils took another spoonful of porridge. "I will need the Creator to help me once again."

Rachel patted her husband's hand. "The Creator always helps."

Nils

As soon as breakfast was over, the shop began to fill with customers. Nils watched Rachel deftly bounce between helping them and assembling lingonberry boughs and wire into a wreath for the front door.

He imagined Leena's dark woolen coat and gloves with holes, her skirt printed with small blue flowers, her leather boots once nice but now scuffed from tramping through the woods. That was all very vivid to him, but he could not see the girl's face.

Experimenting with different facial expressions on small bits of wood resulted in a growing discard pile on the floor. He finished working on the girl's body and then went to the kitchen.

Currently between customers, Rachel was at the table, bent over her wreath. Through its base of fir branches, she'd woven smaller lingonberry pieces. The pop of the red berries throughout the variegated greens matched the ribbon bow she was affixing at the wreath's bottom.

He grabbed a cup of coffee and settled in the cozy warmth of the stove's crackling fire. Needing to seek the Creator, he sat quietly, listening for guidance.

It was several minutes before Rachel stood back from the wreath. "I think I finally have it completed."

Nils continued to stare into the fire, not hearing his wife's next words.

She walked over to him, laying her hand on his shoulder. "Is something wrong?"

He smiled up at her. "I was just seeking the Creator's instructions on how to portray Leena's face. I've tried many times this morning without finding the right look. But He's given me an idea, so I'm to going to try again. Did you need something?"

She squeezed his shoulder. "I'm done with the wreath. When you're done with fika, would you please place it on the door for me?"

"I'll do that right away," Nils said.

As he got up, there was a knock on the back door. He strode to the door and opened it.

"Come in, Klemens." A whoosh of cold air and snow entered with the postman. "It looks like we are in for quite a lot of snow."

Klemens stood on the rug just inside the door. "It does look that way. Vincent asked if I could pick up the carving for Elia. A panicked castle staff is anticipating the early arrival today of all sixteen of the castle's Christmas guests. I agreed to deliver the gift to the castle, as long as that's okay with you."

"Of course. Let me retrieve it." Nils walked into the shop and returned carrying a blue muslin bag.

"I have your mail, Rachel," Klemens was saying as he handed her several letters.

"Thank you. We're hoping for a letter from Stefan. His captain mailed it for him some time ago, but we still haven't received it." She thumbed through the letters, then sighed. "No letter from Stefan. But my sister sent me something." Rachel turned over a red envelope.

"I've carried lots of red envelopes this year," Klemens said.

Nils held out the blue bag. "In here is the carving and the story that goes with it."

"My next stop is the castle." Klemens opened the door. "I better head there before the snow comes down even harder."

"Thank you for delivering the carving." Nils closed the door behind the postman.

Rachel sat down by the fire and opened the red envelope. She held up the front of the card inside, showing Nils a scene of children holding hands and dancing around a Christmas tree with a woman, likely their mother, looking on.

"Oh, Nils! This scene reminds me of my brother and sisters and me as children. We would dance and dance around the tree."

Nils grinned. "We should dance around the tree this year. We're still children at heart." He laughed.

Rachel giggled, then opened the card and read from it aloud.

To Nils, Rachel and Stefan,

Wishes come, and wishes go—
Every Christmas time 'tis so—
None more tender, none more true,
Than this wish of mine to you,
Sent in all regard to say,
Joyous be your Christmas Day!
–Anonymous–
With all our love,
Iris and family

"How beautiful. I can't wait to show this to Stefan." She placed the card on the mantle.

Nils wrapped his arms around her. "Hopefully, he will walk through that door very soon."

Chapter 16

Pip

The woodsman stepped into the clearing with his horse and wagon. Several men were pulling fish from nets in the boats and placing them on a table to be gutted. I flew to the top of a shack for a bird's-eye view. At a large open fire nearby, a hunchbacked man used a long wooden paddle to stir the contents of a large pot.

Anders and the man exchanged hellos. The red-haired girl was emptying a sled of sticks by the fire but did not look up.

"Could I talk with the boss of your operation?" Anders asked.

The man studied the wagon full of wood, then sneered at the sticks by the fire. "Boss!" he yelled. "There's a fellow with wood here asking for you."

A bald man emerged from one of the fishing huts and took long strides toward Anders. "I'm the boss here."

"My name is Anders Dahl. I live a couple of miles from here." Anders pointed to the girl. "I've met your worker there. She was in the woods gathering sticks by my cabin."

"I'm Rolf Selberg," the bald man said, shaking Anders's hand. "Leena is my niece. If she's given you any trouble, I'll take care of that."

Leena looked up and began to tremble visibly, her fear palpable in the air.

"Not at all," Anders reassured him, his voice calm and soothing. "But seeing Leena gave me an idea."

Rolf narrowed his eyes. "And, what's that?"

"I have to make several long trips away from home each week to deliver wood, and my wife needs help with chores and making cheese. Could Leena come work for us for part of each day?"

Leena's head snapped up, her eyebrows knitting together as she looked at Anders. He gave her a wink, but she picked up the handle of the sled and pulled it toward the barn, frowning.

"I can't spare her." Rolf said brusquely, turning back toward his hut. "She has chores to do here."

Anders followed a few paces. "I know she gathers sticks for your fire. What else does she do here?"

Rolf turned half round. "Empties gut buckets into brine barrels, does the animal chores, and other things."

Anders nodded. "I would never suggest the chores here not be done. I'm willing to help Leena do her chores each morning so she can go to my cabin with me and help my wife. The arrangement could work for both of us. You get your work done, and so do I."

Rolf faced Anders but rubbed his chin, his reluctance hanging in the air like a heavy cloud. "I don't know."

Anders motioned to his wagon. "Logs like these on my sled will burn much longer than sticks. I can give you these and bring you a load every few days."

The hunchbacked man eyed the wood with a grin. "Boss, logs would make my job easier. With sticks, I can never keep the fire as hot as we need."

Leena returned from the barn, picked up two full buckets, and lugged them toward the barrels.

"If Leena can stay and work at my cabin into the evening," Anders added, "I can return with her for chores each morning. Of course, I would then be responsible for feeding her."

As she passed Anders, Leena sighed heavily.

Rolf stared at Anders for quite some time. "We can give it a try. The logs will be helpful, and maybe the chores will actually get done correctly." He glared at Leena.

She looked down, her shoulders quivering as she deposited two empty buckets next to the line of full ones beside the gutting table.

"Excellent. Can we get started right away? I need to deliver a load of wood this afternoon, and my wife will appreciate the help."

Rolf looked at the two empty buckets, shrugged, and waved Anders away. "Once all the buckets are empty. If she doesn't behave for you, just have her sleep in the barn. She's used to it." He stalked back to the fishing shack.

"Thanks for the advice," Anders said, looking at Leena. "But I assure you that will never happen," he muttered under his breath.

The hunchbacked man walked up to Anders. "I'll show you where to stack the wood from your wagon."

Anders followed him and quickly unloaded the wood as Leena continued hauling buckets. He tried to get her attention as she went past him, but she trudged along, focusing on the ground before her. Once Anders was done, he picked up two full buckets from the line as Leena also grabbed two more. She looked up, and Anders smiled at her. "Let's do your chores and then gather whatever you want to bring to the cabin."

"I don't have much," she replied stonily. "A box that my father gave me last Christmas and my docka. Mama made her for me."

Once the chores were done, Leena retrieved her belongings from where she'd hidden them under straw in a corner of the barn. The small limewood box had a flower etched on its top. The muslin docka wore a red shirt and a black-and-white-striped skirt. A matching striped scarf circled a face stitched with black thread. Leena tucked the doll under her arm and put the box in her apron pocket.

"Does your docka have a name?" Anders asked tenderly.

"Greta," Leena said.

"A fine name," he said. "Let's head back to the cabin."

The girl beside him, he pulled the sled into the woods as I flew behind them. Once they were a few hundred feet into the woods, he stopped and knelt smiling before her. I perched on a nearby branch.

"Leena, it worked!" he exclaimed. "The Father was right. It worked! Now you can go home with us."

"And then back to work." Leena sighed.

"No, Leena! It won't be work like you've been doing. Sure, you can help Maja with things around the cabin, like you helped your parents in Stockholm. But there will be time for play and learning. You'll be a little girl at our home."

Leena looked up at him, her mouth hanging open, tears filling her wide eyes.

"I will get to play with my docka again?"

"Yes! And with Clara, Tucker, Siv, and our funny goats. They will be happy to have you with us." He extended a hand to her. "Let me help you into the wagon. I'm sorry there's no seat for you, since this wagon is only for hauling wood."

Smiling through her tears, Leena lifted her arms toward him. Returning her smile, Anders picked her up and placed her in the back of the wagon bed. He grabbed Siv's lead and began guiding the entourage to the cabin.

Leena hugged her docka to her chest as they pulled away. I spread my wings to take off for my home, excited to tell my family that the red-haired girl went home with the woodsman. Then I noticed a large greylag goose hiding in a lingonberry bush. Was she watching Anders and the girl? I flitted to a branch beside the bush.

"It's true!" I heard the goose saying to herself. "I can't believe that the man was able to help the wee girl. The ridiculous dog said he could. But who would have ever believed it?"

"You know the hungry girl too?" I asked the goose.

She startled and looked up at me. "Of course I do! I've been her protector the entire time she's been here." Her stern voice softened. "As much as I could anyway. Who are you, and how do you know my girl?"

"I'm Pip. I saw when Leena first asked the woodsman for food. I was gathering seeds for my cache when, all of a sudden, there was movement in the bushes." I filled the goose in on my first encounter with Leena.

"I'm Grendela," the goose told me. "I've lived in the barn with Leena."

"The poor girl," I said. "Sleeping in a barn isn't for humans. I just found out today that the woodsman has a woman who lives with him. She has a happy face, so I'm glad the woodsman was able to convince Leena's uncle to let her stay with them."

"Me, too," the goose added. "I hope it works out for the wee girl. She will be far away from me here, so I can't watch out for her."

Grendela's concern touched my heart. "I could stop in each day at the cabin and then fly here and give you news of Leena."

"Oh, would you?" Grendela's eyes brightened. "That would make me feel better about her leaving here. I could give you news of what happens when she's here at the fishing village. That way, we both will know how the girl fares."

"It's a deal," I told the goose. "I'm off now and will be back tomorrow with my first report."

Chapter 17

Karl

A loud thump woke the duke. *Did that come from Elia's room?* He sprang from his bed.

After several attempts to get his arm through the sleeve of his night coat as he ran, he dropped the coat outside his daughter's door and rushed inside. Elia was sitting up in bed, biting her lip as he burst into the room.

"Are you okay, Elia?" the duke asked.

"I'm sorry, Papa. I was trying to reach one of the carvings on my bedside table and knocked off the book Nanny has been reading to me."

"You're sitting up!" The duke walked to her, picking up the book off the floor. "You are better!" He stumbled as he noticed her smiling at him from the bed.

"Well, I can't miss Christmas, and I have to know how the story ends." Elia's chuckle turned into a coughing fit that racked her small body.

Alma ran into the room. "Beggin' your pardon, Duke. I went to the kitchen for some hot tea and toast for Miss Elia." Rushing to the bed, Elia's nanny held the cup of warm tea to the girl's lips. "Try a bit of this, dear."

The girl sipped the warm liquid. Eventually her coughing subsided.

"I made you my mama's special tea," Alma said, "With honey and some of Brigitta's lemon syrup from the pantry. It helps keep the coughing at bay."

"Well done, Alma," Duchess Sylvie said, entering the room and handing the duke his coat. "That tea did the trick."

"Yes, well done," the duke added, now putting on his coat with ease. He turned to the duchess. "Look at our girl! She is feeling better."

"She is!" said the duchess, smiling.

"The fever broke last night, m'lady." Alma grinned. "Elia is regaining her strength and had me read her the carving story over and over."

"I like to play with the carvings," Elia said, eating a square of toast.

"However," Alma said, "you've been up for quite some time now and need a nap after you're done eating."

"Would you like me to read you to sleep, my dear?" the duke asked. "I have time before breakfast."

"Yes please, Papa. Nanny has been reading me the book of fables you and Mama got me for Christmas last year."

The duchess bent down and kissed Elia. "I will get dressed and see to our guests while you enjoy a story and get some rest."

"Is Grandmamma here?" Elia asked.

"Here and anxious to see you," the duchess answered. "All the family arrived late last night, before the storm. Alma, why don't you go down to the kitchen for breakfast and take the morning off. The duke and I will take turns watching over Elia until lunch."

"Yes, m'lady," Alma curtsied and followed the duchess out of the room.

The duke sat next to Elia. "What carving were you trying to reach when you raised such a ruckus this morning?"

Elia laughed. "I didn't mean to raise a ruckus." She pointed to a carving on the stand. "I wanted to see Leena again. She looks so sad and helpless."

"She does," the duke observed.

"Do you think the woodcutter and his wife can really help her?" Elia asked.

"Only the rest of the story will answer that." The duke tucked Elia's blankets back around her, then thumbed through the book he'd retrieved from the floor. "What fable shall we read?"

"Will you read me the story that came with the carvings instead?" Elia pled.

The duke chuckled. "You aren't tired of hearing that tale?"

"No, Papa!" she exclaimed, smiling when he laughed. "I want to hear it again, please."

Rachel

The delivery boy watched Rachel tie a red ribbon around the package. "Thank you, ma'am, for wrapping my ma's present."

"I'm happy to help. You certainly picked out the perfect tree for us." Rachel looked at the eight-foot-tall spruce in the corner of the shop as she handed the boy his package. "You best get this home before more of this snow comes down. Please wish Christmas blessings to your folks from Herr Kindberg and me."

"I will, ma'am. Thanks again." He waved his mittened hand as he walked out the door.

Nils had not moved from his chair all morning. He was so focused on his work that Rachel doubted he noticed the many customers who had come by despite the bad weather.

She touched his shoulder. "Can I warm your coffee for you, Nils?"

He looked up. "I would appreciate that so much, dear. With just three days till Christmas, I'm trying to finish up several projects."

She brought the kettle from the kitchen and added hot coffee to his cup. "Will you have time to help with the tree this evening, or should I decorate it between customers?"

"Your doing it would probably be best," Nils said, smiling up at her. "Without Stefan here, I have too many orders to finish."

"Of course. I already have all the decorations made, so it won't take me long." She gave him a peck on the cheek and returned the kettle to the stove.

Throughout the afternoon, she waited on a dwindling number of customers braving the storm and added straw angels, Advent stars, saffron pretzels, and candles to the tree. As she finished, she stood back from the tree and turned three-hundred-sixty degrees, viewing the entire shop. The gaiety of the colorful decorations hanging throughout, the candles flickering on the tree, and the scent of cardamom bread baking assured her it would be a very special Christmas—once Stefan made it home.

The bell on the shop door rang a few moments before closing, and a wisp of a man covered in snow stepped inside. He took off the scarf wrapped around his head, releasing powdery snow onto the entry rug.

"Jesper!" Rachel exclaimed. "What are you doing out in this weather? Warm yourself by the fire."

"Did you come for the carving?" Nils asked, getting up from his workbench and joining the castle's footman by the fire.

"Yes. It's been very busy at the castle, and I finally was able to slip away." Jesper rubbed his hands in front of the fire crackling in the grate.

At Rachel's invitation, he sat at the coffee table, where she had earlier placed a tray full of cups and cookies. She darted to the kitchen, returned with the coffee kettle, and filled cups for all three of them. Jesper slurped at the warm liquid.

"I have the carving ready for you," Nils said, returning to his worktable. He grabbed a blue muslin bag and brought the gift back to Jesper.

"May I take a peek?" Jesper asked shyly. "The entire castle is abuzz about the carvings and the story."

Nils chuckled. "I can't see how that would hurt anything." He pulled the carving out of the bag. "This is Maja, the woodcutter's wife."

The carving was of a woman wearing a brown wool dress over a long-sleeved muslin shirt, as well as a white cotton apron and a blue scarf. Her smile was so wide it spread across her whole face, making Rachel smile too as she viewed the figurine.

"That will be quite the addition." Jesper finished slurping his coffee.

"How is Elia doing?" Rachel asked, filling his cup once again.

"Still coughing some but better than she was. She had tea and toast for breakfast and soup for lunch."

"That is welcome news." Nils turned the carving over in his hands. "I will wrap this up for you."

"Yes, Jesper, you better get back." Rachel peered out the shop window. "The snow is piling rapidly on the wooden sidewalks."

"Nils, Vincent also wanted me to tell you something." Jesper paused, looking uncomfortable.

"Is there a concern?" Nils asked, handing the footman the carving, wrapped against the weather with a second, canvas bag.

"The last of the visitors arrived at the castle late this afternoon. They said that the trains have stopped running due to heavy snow. With the storm still raging, the engineers didn't know when the trains would be running again."

Rachel looked away, brushing sudden tears from her eyes.

"Please tell Vincent I appreciate him letting us know," Nils said.

"I will. Thank you for the carving, and Merry Christmas to you both." Jesper stepped out onto the snowy street and closed the door behind him.

Nils turned to Rachel and opened his arms to envelop her. She began to weep.

"We have no idea where Stefan is or if he is safe," Rachel cried. "And now he has no way to get home to us."

Chapter 18

Maja

"Here you go, ladies." Maja chuckled as she locked the goats in their pen in the barn. She picked up a pail of milk and headed back to the cabin to finish dinner. The last few weeks had been pure bliss. Having a child in the home again was helping to heal the pain from losing her son. Nothing would ever take the ache away entirely, but being able to care for Leena had somehow made it bearable.

Rounding the corner of the cabin, Maja heard crunching in the snow. The horse and wagon came into view through the bushes. *Anders and Leena are home!* Maja's heart lifted and then dropped. She could tell by their faces that something was wrong.

Anders stopped Siv in front of the cabin, helping Leena down from the wagon.

"Leena, what's wrong?" Maja asked, noticing the girl's tearstained face as she rushed past and into the cabin.

"What's happened?" Maja asked Anders. "Things have been going well these past few weeks, haven't they?"

Anders didn't answer. Instead, he took Maja's hand as he grabbed Siv's lead and headed to the barn.

Inside the barn, Anders removed the harness from the horse and spoke softly. "Leena's uncle informed me that they're leaving to return to their village at the end of the week."

"Oh no!" Maja sighed. "We knew they would have to return sometime. I guess we were so wrapped up in Leena being with us, we forgot." She swallowed hard as she scooped grain into Siv's feeder.

"Yes, we knew. But when Leena heard him say it, she was terribly upset, sobbing uncontrollably as soon as we were in the woods and away from her uncle. I tried to console her, though I still have no idea how to keep her here with us." Anders's voice was filled with worry.

Maja slipped her hand into his again. "We may not know the way, but the Father does. Just as He showed you how to help Leena the first time, He can show you how to convince her uncle to let her stay with us over the winter."

"I've been asking the Father. But what if His answer is no? What if she won't be able to live with us anymore?" Anders's voice softened as Siv nuzzled his arm. "Leena has thrived here. She finally feels safe."

"I can't believe that the Father would let her stay with us just to have her go back to her uncle. We just have to wait for the Father's answer." Maja pressed her lips into a determined line.

"We only have a few days, so let's pray together," Anders said. Holding both of Maja's hands, he bowed his head. "Father, You know how dear Leena is to us, and we know she is precious to You. Please help us know what to say to her uncle so she can stay with us through the winter—or even, if somehow possible, always and forever. We need Your direction, Father. May we hear Your voice."

"Amen," Maja said. She hugged Anders. "I better go check on Leena. I made a new dress for her docka from some scraps of fabric. Maybe that will cheer her up."

Leena

Leena slept fitfully all night. She lay in her bed talking to her docka. "We are going to have to go back with Uncle again, Greta. I am glad you will be with me. Without you, I have no one."

A ray of sunshine peeked through the window. Leena threw back the warm covers and dressed quickly. The cabin was quiet, and when she stepped into the kitchen, no one was there. She put on her coat, hat, and mittens and headed to the barn.

As she opened the barn door, she saw Maja leading a goat to the milking stand.

"Good morning, Leena. You're up early." Maja smiled warmly.

"I couldn't sleep," Leena said, noticing several pails of milk lined up along the wall. "That is a lot of milk!"

"Today is cheese day. I'm milking the goats so that I have enough milk and whey to make a couple of batches." Maja positioned the goat in the stand. "This is Lotti."

"Hello, Lotti," Leena said, admiring the rich, walnut-colored undercoat that showed on the goat's face and legs. She had a caramel-colored torso, a white triangle tuft on her forehead, two curved horns on top of her head, and a brown wattle of hair that hung beneath her chin.

Maja began to fill the pail with the goat's milk. "Lotti's the first goat we purchased when we came to live at the cabin. She's special. A landrace breed. Very hardy and a great milk producer. That's her kid over in the corner. He was born twelve weeks ago and has just been weaned. Lotti has helped to increase our herd by giving us many kids."

Leena looked into the small pen next to Siv's stall. Curled up in the corner was a tiny goat that eyed her closely. "He looks just like his mother, except for the white feet."

"You can go in the pen if you like," Maja said, the rhythm of the milk hitting the bucket making a song all its own. "Just make sure to close the gate."

Leena stepped into the pen, and the wee goat jumped up and began hopping sideways. She laughed at his antics until the kid ran straight toward her at full speed. The girl pulled back, and the kid skidded to a stop. Leena took a deep breath and slowly reached out her hand to pet him.

"What's his name?" she asked, scratching behind his ears.

"We haven't given him a name yet." Maja released Lotti from the harness. "Would you like to name him?"

"Can I?" Leena asked excitedly. The small goat jumped back and bounced around the pen again.

Maja nodded. "Do you have any ideas of what to name him?"

"Could we call him Kola?" Leena asked as Maja opened the gate to let Lotti into the pen. "He looks like the caramels my mama used to make for Christmas."

Maja giggled. "He *does* look like a caramel. The name Kola is perfect. After I milk two more goats, I'll be ready to head to the cabin."

"You need all this milk for cheese?" Leena asked.

"I'm going to make several batches of hard cheese. Then, with the leftover whey, I'll make gjetost."

"What's that?"

"A soft cheese that's a caramel color."

"Like Kola?" Leena asked.

"Exactly like Kola." Maja chuckled. "I use my great-grandma's recipe, and since not everyone has wonderful goats like ours, I'll make several batches to sell in town."

"May I help?" Leena asked as she closed the gate of the pen.

"If you like. But I must warn you—it requires lots of stirring." Maja tucked a piece of Leena's hair behind her ear. "I don't want you to be worn out. I won't make gjetost till after you get home from doing chores at the fishing village."

"I don't get tired like I used to," Leena said. "Anders helps me."

"Alright. We'll take turns stirring the whey into gjetost. That way it's not too much for either of us."

Anders appeared at the barn door. "Leena, it's time to head to the fishing village."

A quiet sadness swept between them all.

"I don't want to go with Uncle back to Söderhamn," Leena said, tears in her eyes.

"We know, Leena. We don't want you to go, either," Anders said gently. "We've asked the Father to help us find a way to keep you with us this winter."

"Does your Father know how to help?" Leena said, stifling a sob.

Maja stroked Leena's hair and pulled her close. "Yes, dear. He knows everything and wants to help us."

Kola

I stood by my mother in our pen, staring at the weeping girl who, just moments ago, had been playing with me. "Momma, why is the girl so sad?"

"She doesn't have a mother," Momma replied.

"No mother? Does she have a father?"

"No father either," Momma answered. "Several nights ago, Anders and Maja were talking by my stall. It seems Leena's parents have died, and she is living in the fishing village with her uncle, who does not want her and is unkind to her."

"What will Leena do?" I asked. "Can you be her mother?"

"No, son." Momma laughed, then sighed as she watched Leena in Maja's embrace. "She will need human parents, and our caretakers are going to try to help her."

"I hope they can, Momma. Leena is fun to play with."

Chapter 19

Vincent

The comforting aroma of pork-filled palt dumplings wafted through the castle as Vincent arranged the serving dishes on the sideboard in the expansive dining room. His gaze wandered to the two footmen diligently polishing silverware next to each of the table settings. The utensils reflected light from the two ornate chandeliers above the long, dark wooden table.

Brigitta walked steadily into the dining room, carrying a two-foot-high, three-foot-long gingerbread Örebro Rådhus made of multiple cookies and white frosting. The confectionery, a replica of the city's three-story town hall, featured a green ironwork railing, spires at the top, and over a hundred red-trimmed windows. A breathtaking sight, the Christmas centerpiece was a tradition symbolizing the Vasa family's deep-rooted love and pride for their city.

"I've made space for your masterpiece right here," Vincent said as he directed his wife to the spot. "Well done, dear! Even more spectacular than last year."

"Thank you." Brigitta smiled and paused briefly before taking a deep breath and pretending to wipe sweat from her brow. "Now back to the kitchen to clean up and prepare for the next meal."

Vincent chuckled at her gesture. "It's a bustling time, but what a joy to hear the castle resounding with laughter once again."

"Indeed, it is," Brigitta agreed. "Elia has asked for porridge. Would you have time to take it up to her before lunch is served?"

"Of course! Let me give the footmen directions for their next task, then I'll be down to the kitchen to pick up the tray."

Vincent soon walked up the stairs with a tray bearing porridge, milk, and honey. He heard voices from inside Elia's bedroom and waited in the doorway, not wanting to interrupt.

"Grandmamma, this is Leena, the poor girl who lost her parents and was sleeping in a barn." Elia handed the carving to the petite, grey-haired countess sitting on the edge of the bed. "And this is Maja, the woodsman's wife. She just came back from taking care of her ill sister."

"These carvings are very beautiful," said Countess Pernilla.

"They aren't just carvings, Grandmamma. They are part of a story. The tale of Leena, a scared orphan girl, and Anders, a kind man who wants to help her. He is asking his Father how to help Leena but no one knows how that will happen."

Vincent chose that moment to quietly enter. His heart warmed, because the girl was getting better.

"Miss Elia, Brigitta sent up porridge for you." Vincent set the tray on the table. He bowed to the duchess's mother.

"Hello, Vincent," the countess said with a smile. She turned to Elia. "That looks delicious, dear. May I add honey to the porridge for you?"

"Two spoonfuls, please," Elia said.

The countess laughed. "It seems someone is feeling much better."

"Vincent, is the tree up in the drawing room?" Elia asked.

"Yes, miss. It has been placed in its usual spot, and decorations for it will be made this afternoon."

Elia slurped her tea. "Has Brigitta finished the gingerbread house?"

"It is done and in its place of honor on the sideboard in the dining room." Vincent stoked the fire and retrieved some empty dishes from the bedside table.

"I can't wait to see it!" Elia smiled enthusiastically. "I'm going to ask Mama if I can go down," she said to her grandmother as Vincent walked out of the room.

Elia

That afternoon, Papa wrapped Elia in several blankets and carried her down the stairs.

"Can you take me to see the gingerbread house?" she asked as they reached the main floor.

"I think we can manage a bit of a detour." Entering the dining room, Papa smiled when the magnificence of the confectionery made Elia gasp.

"Oh, Papa! Have you ever seen such a wonder?" He chuckled while she exclaimed over every detail of the ornate house.

Mama entered the room. "I was wondering where the two of you were."

"I couldn't wait to see the gingerbread house," said Elia.

"Brigitta's work is lovely," said Mama, caressing Elia's cheek and then touching Papa's arm. "Our family guests are waiting in the drawing room."

As Papa carried Elia down the hall, she grinned at hearing familiar voices laughing and talking. When they entered the drawing room, full of plush furnishings, her twin cousins shouted her name and waved for her to join the family around a large table in the center of the room. Vincent winked at her from the hearth, where he was stoking the fire.

After hovering over Papa as he sat Elia in a chair, Mama tucked blankets around Elia's legs. "There you go darling. Are you warm enough?"

"Yes. I can't wait to make decorations." Elia looked toward the twelve-foot tree standing in front of the floor-length window on the room's south wall.

"Let us know if you get tired," Mama said. "We don't want you to wear yourself out."

"Don't worry, love," Papa said to Mama. "I'll keep a close eye on our girl. If she shows any signs of fatigue, I'll carry her upstairs for a rest."

Elia chatted with her cousins as the adults laid out strips of paper in various colors and patterns, along with glue. After an hour of merriment, a colorful array of Advent stars covered the end of the table. While the glue on the stars dried, Grandmamma added a ribbon to each, so they could be hung on the tree and placed in the windows.

Auntie then skillfully fashioned straw people, one to represent each family member. Elia watched her tie red yarn around vertical straw bundles to delineate necks, wrists, and ankles, creating miniature versions to represent the children and various shapes and sizes for the adults. Elia's older cousin used felt and thread to sew red hats, dresses, and other clothing. Once finished, the crafters lined up the straw people for family members to guess which was theirs. After everyone claimed their miniature, the straw creations were added to the large evergreen.

Elia oohed and aahed as the Advent stars and other decorations were carefully placed on the tree. Papa opened the old box of Swedish flags, a wedding gift from his parents, and began hanging the flags throughout the branches.

"In every home tonight, our nation's flag adorns Christmas trees to remind us of our great country," he said. Then he turned to look at Elia. "Living in Sweden is but one of the special gifts we have this holiday season."

Elia wished she could help Mama and Grandmamma clip the small candles on the outside edge of the branches. Vincent would light them on Christmas Eve, just before the family came in to sing Christmas carols.

"May I put my Advent star on the tree?" Elia asked excitedly. Her parents looked at each other. Finally, Elia saw Mama give a nod.

"I'll carry you over," Papa said, picking Elia up. She tucked her multicolored Advent star front and center in the decorated evergreen.

"That is perfect, my dear," Grandmamma said.

"Now it's time for you to rest," Papa whispered to Elia.

"Can I please stay till the dancing begins?"

"We will wait to do that after you're rested, child," Grandmamma said. "There's no hurry. With that storm raging outside, we won't have our normal visitors tonight."

Elia turned to the windows, which were covered with snow and ice. She'd been so busy making decorations that she hadn't heard the storm.

"Look, Papa! The windows have crystal pictures on them." Her voice filled with wonder. "Each one of them is so different."

"Truly magical," Papa added as he picked her up. "Now off to rest. You can return later if you feel up to it."

"I will, Papa. I'm feeling much better." Elia stifled a yawn.

Papa giggled. "I am happy to hear that," he said, carrying her to her room.

Once tucked in, Elia gathered her carvings on her bed, glancing at each character until she came to Leena. "My hope is that Anders and Maja find a way to help you, Leena. Every girl should have a home and someone to love them." Elia tucked the carving under the covers with her. "And a happy Christmas," she whispered as she dozed off to sleep.

Chapter 20

Tucker

When Anders harnessed Siv to the wagon after breakfast, I noticed Clara was sleeping under the chair outside the door again. I decided to sneak up on her, so I crawled toward her slowly on my belly.

"Don't you even think about it, Tucker McGinty," she said without opening her eyes.

I stopped short. "What do you mean? I'm not doing anything except preparing to go on a super-important mission with my master. I will know before anyone else what plan Anders got from his Father."

"You won't be the first to know," she said, licking her paw. "I heard Anders tell the plan to Maja in the cabin last night. Too bad you aren't allowed in there."

"I don't believe you," I said, shaking my head.

"Believe what you want, dog, but here comes Maja with part of the plan."

Maja emerged from the cabin with a linen-wrapped bundle. She approached the wagon, where Leena was standing, and handed the package to Anders.

"This and my prayers go with you both," Maja said, buttoning Leena's coat. "I am glad I got those two new buttons sewed on your coat before it got colder."

"We will both be home by lunchtime," Anders said.

"Hopefully." Leena sighed as Anders picked her up and put her in the wagon.

"Our Father gave us a plan," Maja said reassuringly, "so now we have to believe it will work."

Leena held on to her belongings with tears in her eyes as Anders picked up Siv's lead rope and clicked his tongue for the horse to move. "Come on, Tucker McGinty," Anders said. "We need to get going."

The trip to the fishing village was somber. There was no chatter like other times, only the sound of the wagon wheels crunching over the packed snow. Once Anders stopped Siv, I looked back as he was taking Leena down from the wagon. He bent down on one knee and hugged her tightly.

"We will get all the chores done first," he told her. "Then I will speak with your uncle."

She wiped tears from her eyes. "I don't think Uncle will change his mind. He expects me to go with him today, so I can work and pay my way."

Anders reached into the wagon and held up the bundle Maja gave him. "This may convince your uncle to let you stay with us."

Leena and Anders entered the clearing, dodging several men scurrying to pack barrels of fish, supplies, and smaller animals onto a longboat.

"Get a move on, men," Leena's uncle barked. "We need to load the ships and leave before this weather changes."

About to follow Anders into the clearing, I heard movement from a nearby stand of bushes and trees. Approaching the stand stealthily, I found Grendela squawking up at a small bird in a tree.

"Are you talking to that bird?" I asked.

"None of your business," Grendela said. "I see you're back. Today is a sad day. We'll be leaving soon, and I was hoping the girl would get to stay with your master."

"Don't worry. My master has a plan." I puffed out my chest.

"I heard," Grendela said, looking back at the bird.

"You look familiar," I said, eyeing the bird. "Have you been at the cabin?"

"Many times," the bird answered. "I've seen you there."

"He's been bringing me reliable reports, unlike you." Grendela scowled and then turned to the bird. "Thanks again, Pip. If you stop back by in a while, I'll fill you in on what's happened." The bird flew off, and Grendela paced before me.

"Do you know what your master's plan is?"

"I'm not sure," I told her. "It can't be giving more wood, as my master's supply is very low. I heard him tell his wife he would need to cut wood for weeks to fill the orders he has."

"The poor lass needs a real home where she can be a child, not a servant." Grendela sighed, walking toward the barn. "This is likely goodbye. I'll try to help the girl all I can."

"My master has a plan," I called after her. "You'll see. Leena will come home with us."

Anders

After tying Siv and the wagon at the edge of the clearing, Anders took Leena's hand and gave it a squeeze.

"Good, you're here," Rolf shouted at them. "We need all hands for packing up. Men, take half of this wood and put it on the longboat. We'll use it once we get ashore at home. Girl, run to the barn and feed the rest of the animals, then get back here to me. I have things for you to haul to the boat."

"I can help," Anders offered. Not waiting for Rolf's answer, the woodsman quickly grabbed a stack of nets and headed toward the boat. Leena headed to the barn to feed the animals.

Throughout the morning, Anders helped the fishermen make quick work of packing, anxiously realizing he was running out of time. When Rolf paused from shouting to check over his supply list, Anders grabbed Maja's bundle from his wagon and approached the fisherman.

"May we speak for a moment in private?" Anders asked.

"If you make it snappy. I want to make sail today." Rolf led Anders to one of the shanties now deserted.

Anders closed his eyes a moment and prayed silently before he began. "I know you're planning on Leena going with you, but my wife and I are wondering if we could keep the girl with us to work at our place. We need the help, and our care would save you the cost of her keep."

Rolf stared coldly at Anders. "I'd be losing out on the girl working and helping at home."

"I thought of that," Anders said, holding up Maja's bundle. "In exchange for the work Leena would do for you, I brought gjetost cheese we've made." He opened the linen-wrapped package. "This cheese brings top dollar at the mercantile, and I have twenty-four blocks of it with me. I'll give it to you as payment for the girl working for us throughout the winter and until you return next year."

"Gjetost!" Rolf exclaimed. "We don't have that in our village, but it is very popular with the people. I could make a nice profit off that."

He took out his knife and cut off a piece.

"Great quality," he said, savoring the bite. "You know, I never wanted the girl. I never cared for my brother or his snooty wife, and it's just like him to stick me with his brat."

Anders bristled, thankful Leena was not in earshot.

"But there's money promised to me for taking care of her till she's of age, so I don't think—"

"We're not interested in any money," Anders said. "Just help on the farm. You're the uncle. You have the right to that money, not us."

Rolf eyed Anders. "I'm not sure I'll be back this way next year, but we might be able to make a deal. If you had, say, forty-eight blocks of gjetost, I might be willing to let you keep the girl. Permanently."

"Deal!" Anders exclaimed, reaching out to shake Rolf's hand. "I'll return to my cabin and retrieve the remaining blocks before you sail."

"Perfect," Rolf said. "Easy money in my pocket, and no brat to take care of." Whistling, he walked out of the shanty and back toward the shore.

Anders hurried from the shanty, frantically searching for Leena. He finally found her in the barn.

"Let's go, Leena," he said. "We need to move fast."

Chapter 21

Nils

Nils added three more logs to the kitchen fire, filling the room with comforting warmth. Outside, winds howled over Lake Hjälmaren, as the blizzard blanketed the landscape in a thick layer of snow.

He went to the stove, poured a cup of rich coffee, and sat before the fire. Nils cherished these tranquil moments nestled in the house, so sublimely serene.

"Good morning, my Creator," Nils prayed. "I thank You for guiding my hands and bringing joy and encouragement through the gift You have given me. I wait upon You this morning for direction, guidance, and inspiration."

Though told by many that he had a unique relationship with the Creator, Nils knew that wasn't true. As a young man, he'd observed his father sitting silently for long periods.

"Papa," he said one day, "what are you doing when sitting quietly like that?"

"Seeking the Creator's guidance on what to make and how to make it," his father explained. "That direction is what enables my carving to bring joy to others."

"You can hear the Creator?" Nils had asked incredulously.

"Of course. He loves to talk with us, but you have to be quiet and listen in order to hear Him."

Intrigued by that revelation, Nils began sitting quietly himself. He would close his eyes and talk to the Creator as if to a friend, then wait expectantly for an answer. The insight he gained from the Creator during those moments deepened their connection and brought Nils a sense of peace, even on a stormy morning like this.

Nils stood and poured another cup of coffee, studying the crystal images decorating the windows.

"Good morning, my love," Rachel said, walking into the kitchen and putting on her apron. "Happy Christmas Eve. I see the snow has not stopped." She sighed. "I hope Stefan is somewhere safe and warm."

"That is my prayer as well," Nils replied, hugging her. "I have several items that need to be delivered. However, this storm may make that impossible."

"I have the Modine family's gifts and food to deliver as well," Rachel said, placing another box of cookies into a basket on the chair by the table. "It seems we must wait for the storm to subside before making our deliveries. Until then, why don't you show me your latest creation for Elia?"

Nils picked up two small carvings of grey alder and placed them on the table. "This is Lotti and Kola, a landrace goat and her kid who belong to Anders and Maja."

"What a fine pair!" Rachel said. "The intricate details make these carvings special—the hay in Kola's mouth and the sweet way Lotti's head turns toward him when he's placed before her. You have perfectly captured the look of a mother's love on Lotti's face."

"Jesper will be here soon, could you place them in the bag?"

"Of course," Rachel said, gently adding the carvings to the muslin bag. "Are these the last carvings for Elia?"

"No. I've already begun on what I believed was the last one. However, there will be one more after that." Nils turned to write something on the kraft paper tablet he kept on the table.

Rachel

Rachel had seen Nils with that far-off look before. He was deep in thought, his mind filled with the images of his next creation. She had figured out long ago that it was best not to ask too many questions when Nils was creating.

Determined to make the holiday memorable for them, Rachel rinsed a ham and patted it dry before placing it in a pan to slowly roast. Later, she would smother the ham with a mixture of egg, grainy mustard, and brown sugar, topped with crushed gingerbread cookies.

She took stock of what she'd already finished to put on their festive Christmas julbord table—oatmeal with a herring marinade, two kinds of sausages, jellies, and saffron buns. The lutefisk was soaking, and now the ham was in the oven. Next, she needed to cut and bake a batch of gingerbread cookies from the dough she stirred up last night. She began to hum "Now Are Lit a Thousand Christmas Candles" as she rolled out the gingerbread. Nils soon sang along from his workbench, in his rich baritone voice.

A thousand Christmas candles are now being lit
Around the dark sphere of the earth
With thousands and thousands of light beams as well
On the deep blue bank of the sky
And through city and country tonight
The joyful message of Christmas is now being carried
That born is the lord Jesus Christ
Our savior and God

Rachel added her alto voice to his as he joined her in the kitchen.

Oh you, the star over Bethlehem
Let your soft light
Light up with hope and peace
Into every home and house
In every heart lonely and dark
Carry a gentle light beam
A beam of God's lovingly light
In sacred Christmas time

"I've always loved that song," Rachel said, smiling. "The snow is going to keep away most of our customers today," she observed. "Would you like to decorate gingerbread cookies with me once you're done carving?"

"I would love to. I'm almost done with the Dahl cabin, and I can work on Elia's final piece after we've decorated."

Rachel rolled out the dough and used a knife to draw stars, bells, and hearts from it. Shortly, the sweet, spicy aroma of cookies filled the kitchen, adding to the festive atmosphere.

As she and Nils used white icing to decorate the rich golden gingerbread, the afternoon hours passed. The storm outside continued, snow and wind persisting into the evening, when Nils placed the star on the top of the tree. "I believe the new Advent stars you made this year are a wonderful addition."

Rachel smiled. "I can't take all the credit. The Modine children made some of them."

"You don't say," Nils said, looking over the tree. "They did a nice job. Are we ready to light the candles?"

"Oh yes! I'll blow out all the other lights in the house."

The twinkle of the candlelight cast tiny prisms on the windows as Nils and Rachel stood together holding hands.

"It is a beautiful tree," she said, sadness creeping into her voice. "I hope Stefan will make it home in time to see it."

"Me too. Tonight, however, it is just the two of us, and I believe we talked about dancing around this tree together." A twinkle in his eye, Nils grabbed her hands and sang.

Now it's Christmas time again!
Now it's Christmas time again!

They danced several times around the lighted evergreen, until they fell into a heap on the couch, out of breath and giggling like children. Darkness had already fallen outside, and the house began to chill. Nils added more wood to the fire.

"I will get supper ready for us," Rachel said as she walked to the kitchen. "It will only take a few minutes."

"Perfect," Nils said. "I'm hungry."

She laughed. "You're always hungry."

Nils sat at the table, watching Rachel spoon ham drippings into two bowls. Already on the table were sliced cheeses, and limpa bread, made of dark rye flour, caraway, molasses, and candied fruit.

"I look forward to this every year." Nils took a piece of limpa bread and soaked it in the ham drippings.

"I have gingerbread cookies for us to enjoy with our fika afterward," Rachel said.

"Wife, you do spoil me."

"I love to spoil my family," she said. "I just wish *all* of our family was here."

Nils took her hands in his. "How about we pray for Stefan before we start to eat?"

"I would like that," she said.

He squeezed her hands and closed his eyes. "Creator, You know where our Stefan is, and we pray he is safe and with others who are celebrating this time of joy. Please bring him home to us and, until then, protect him wherever he is."

"Amen," Rachel said quietly, wishing she had the same confidence Nils seemed to have. Her latest dreams were full of nightmares about Stefan. Would they see their son again? Would he come home to them?

Chapter 22

Leena

Leena held fast to Anders's hand, her face brushed by leaves as they raced through bushes and into the woods. Once the wagon was out of sight of the fishing village, Anders stopped Siv and began dancing around. Leena stood by the wagon, watching the woodsman's odd behavior.

"You did it, Father!" the woodsman exclaimed. "You were right!" Anders picked Leena up and twirled her around.

"What's happening?" Leena asked as he put her down. "Don't I need to stay at the fishing village? They are going to sail soon. I still have work to do before I leave with Uncle."

"You don't have to go with your uncle," Anders said with a broad smile. "You get to stay with Maja and me."

"I-I don't understand. My uncle said I had to pay my way." *I prepared my heart to return to Uncle. Now Anders is saying I don't have to go. That can't be so.* "You're sure I can live with you?"

"I am. The plan was to tempt your uncle with some of Maja's cheese in return for you staying with us for the winter. That worked, and then—"

"So I can stay the whole winter?" Leena inquired.

Anders knelt before her. "Not just for the winter, Leena. You can stay with us forever!"

Leena took a step back, shaking her head.

"Your uncle held out until we made a deal about the money he was promised for taking care of you. Once that was done, he decided you could live with us forever." Anders beamed. "My Father was right. He knew all along just the way to work this out."

Leena looked blankly at Anders, her mind not comprehending what she was hearing. She felt as if a tidal wave burst from her heart. A sob escaped her lips, followed by a watershed of tears running down her face.

Anders looked shocked and quickly wrapped her in his arms. "There, there. Let's get you in the wagon." He picked Leena up and placed her in a corner of the wagon, handing her most precious belongings to her and wrapping a blanket around her.

Leena held tightly to Greta and the box her father had given her, trying to make herself believe what Anders had told her, but all she could do was taste the salty tears flowing down her face. *Uncle said no one would ever want me. Now I will live with Anders and Maja? Am I asleep, dreaming in my bed in the cabin?*

Anders led Siv back to the cabin, turning around to check on Leena often as they went. "Father, help Leena feel Your comfort and peace now," he said softly. "She is safe, and I pray she will know that."

A wisp of billowing smoke rose above the bushes in front of them.

"Look, Leena! We're almost home." Anders smiled back at her.

Home. It will be so lovely to have a home again. A warm place to sleep, food to eat, and maybe even a family. "Thank you for wanting me," Leena said when Anders again looked back at the wagon.

He stopped the horse and walked back to her.

"Of course we want you. We love you, Leena, and want you to live with us." Anders squeezed her hand.

She jumped up and buried her face in his woolen coat as the woodsman reached his large arms around her, kissing the top of her head.

"Life will be much better now, I assure you. Maja will be waiting, so we best keep moving." Anders returned to the lead and clicked to signal Siv to move on once again.

Peace washed over Leena's heart as she watched the smoke from the cabin get closer and closer. She craned her neck, keeping her eyes on the stone chimney until, finally, the entire cabin came into view.

There it was. Her home! Rough-hewn timbers stacked one on top of the other, ends notched perfectly and chinking tucked between the rows to keep them warm. Clara was sitting on the wooden chair, Lotti and Kola were in the pen by the barn, and Maja was standing inside the large wooden door—all welcoming Leena *home*.

Maja

Standing in the doorway, Maja was overjoyed when she saw the girl inside the wagon. Leena was going to be with them for Christmas and through the winter. Delight spread over Maja like molasses over porridge. When they reached the front door, she could see the girl's tearstained face and looked at Anders inquiringly.

As Anders took Leena out of the wagon, the girl said shyly, "I get to live with you now."

Maja wrapped her arms around Leena, laughing joyfully. "That is wonderful news! Welcome home, Leena! Let's get inside where it's warm." Maja took Leena's mitten-covered hand.

"I'll need to return to the fishing village, my dear," Anders told her. "Would you help me in the barn for a moment?"

Maja knelt before Leena. "I have a surprise for you in your room. Go ahead in, and I will be right there."

Leena ran into the house, her docka Greta tucked under her arm.

"What's wrong?" Maja asked as Anders picked up a bucket of water and put it in front of Siv for drinking.

"The Father was right. Leena's uncle loved the cheese. It seemed to help warm him to the idea of her staying with us. But as we feared, the money that he was promised came up. I reassured him we would bear the costs of raising Leena—that he could keep the money promised once she turned eighteen."

"What did he say?" Maja held her breath. "Can she stay all winter?"

"He wants an additional twenty-four blocks of gjetost." Anders shook his head. "I was so glad Leena was nowhere near us when he traded her for some cheese."

"You told him he could have it, right?" Maja said anxiously.

"Of course I did, dear. Leena is worth anything we could give. However, I have not told you everything." Anders grasped her trembling hands in his. "Her uncle has agreed to let Leena live with us permanently."

"Permanently?" Maja asked, her legs weakening. "Forever?"

"Yes, my darling. Forever. She is our little girl now." Anders enveloped Maja in his arms.

"Oh, praise to the Father!" Maja whispered, tears streaming down her face.

Clara

I was sitting on the wooden chair outside the cabin door, purring and basking in the gaiety of Leena coming to live with us, when I noticed Tucker McGinty pacing back and forth, muttering to himself.

"Tucker, what is the problem?" I asked. "Leena is here, and all is well.

He huffed. "Not everything is well. I was there when Anders talked to the uncle. He'd take the milk right out of your tea and come back for the sugar, the rogue. Not only has Anders given him all the wood he cut for town orders, but now the uncle wants another twenty-four blocks of gjetost cheese. That's all the blocks Anders and Maja have! I know because I was there when Maja was counting the blocks after making a batch last week."

I studied Tucker and considered the words he'd said. "Why is giving all the blocks a problem?" I asked finally.

"Think, cat!"

Though I bristled at the implied insult, I let it go because Tucker's voice was heavy with concern. He was clearly thinking about more than just himself for a change.

"If the master and mistress have no wood or cheese to sell," Tucker explained, "how will they and Leena—and we—make it through the winter?"

Chapter 23

Rachel

Rachel woke to Nils's soft snoring. He'd been up until the wee hours, finishing Stefan's gift and Elia's final two pieces. The blizzard had raged outside all night, the wind howling and the snow piling up against the buildings. If only the storm would pass so the town could have Christmas.

As she awakened even more, Rachel realized there was no noise, no banging of the wind. She hopped out of bed and opened the wooden window coverings. Sunlight streamed into the room.

"Thank you, Creator!" A laugh of relief escaped her as she realized the storm had finally passed.

"What's going on, wife?" Nils asked, rolling over in the bed.

"The storm has stopped. Look! The sun is out!"

Nils joined her by the window. "Well, it surely is. I better get my warm clothes on and scoop snow from around the front door and sidewalks. Everyone will be coming to the shop to pick up their orders."

Rachel walked to the bureau to brush her hair and get dressed. "I'll make you a hot breakfast. Then, once the snow is cleared, I'm off to call on the Modines before church, which I'm sure will be late today due to the snow."

"I'll find out the time of the Christmas service for us while you run your errands," Nils said.

After breakfast, Rachel bundled the baked goods and gifts for the Modine family. She and the delivery boy who had delivered her tree loaded her baskets onto his sled and braced themselves for the bitter winter air. The sun was shining, but it had not warmed the air much, as the wind was coming off the lake.

Rachel smiled as she saw the Advent stars the children had made hanging in the windows of the Modine home, their bright colors adding to the festive atmosphere. She knocked on the door, the sound echoing in the quiet, snow-covered street.

"Hello, Frau Kindberg. Please come in out of the cold." Fionda shivered from the icy breeze.

"Jarl," Rachel called, "could you take the packages from the delivery boy?"

"Yes, Frau Kindberg," Jarl said, already gathering the packages.

Rachel gave the delivery boy a five-krona coin. "Thank you so much for your help," she told him.

“Thank you, ma’am! That is most generous.” The delivery boy smiled broadly and scurried out the door.

“Are these for us?” Ina asked breathlessly.

“Ina, it’s not polite to ask for things,” Fionda reprimanded.

“I don’t mind. It’s Christmas!” Rachel smiled at Ina, shook the snow from her boots at the door, and set the basket she was carrying in the sitting room. “Merry Christmas, everyone! And yes, Ina, the packages are for you. These boxes are treats and food, so let’s help your mother carry them into the kitchen.” Rachel took off her mittens and gave packages to Jarl, Janna, and Frederick.

Fionda’s eyes filled with tears. Squeezing Fionda’s hand, Rachel whispered, “The Creator provides when we have needs.”

Fionda wiped her tears and helped Frederick with a teetering box of sausages. The merriment brought Fionda’s husband out of the bedroom. Charles was using two canes to stabilize his movements as he walked to a chair.

“What’s going on out here?” he asked with a broad smile.

“Frau Kindberg brought us some treats,” Jarl said over his shoulder as he walked to the kitchen.

“And presents,” Ina added gleefully.

Once they returned to the sitting room, the children noticed Rachel take six red packages out of the basket she was carrying and place them on the table.

“What are those packages?” Fredrick asked.

"I found them on my doorstep this morning. I'm not sure where they came from." Rachel winked at Fionda. "But they were marked with your names, so I figured I'd better deliver them right away."

"Look, this one has your name, Ina," Janna said, handing her the package.

Ina squealed, her eyes lighting up with joy. The rest of the children raced over to the table, their faces filled with excitement and anticipation.

"Mama, Papa, there are gifts for you too!" Janna exclaimed.

"Well, I will leave you to the opening. I need to get home." Rachel put on her mittens again.

"Children, what do we tell Frau Kindberg?" Charles said, turning to Rachel and mouthing his own thank-you over the children's heads.

"Thank you!" the children sang out in one big chorus.

"You're most welcome," Rachel said, picking up her basket.

Ina rushed over to Rachel and hugged her knees.

"Merry Christmas, Frau Kindberg!" the girl said joyfully, looking up at Rachel.

"Oh, Merry Christmas to you too, dear Ina." Rachel bent down to return the hug. "You'd better go open your gift before church starts."

Ina ran back to the table, where the other children were opening their gifts.

"I must hurry along so I am ready when the church bells ring," Rachel said as she walked out the door. "See you there, children." Although she wouldn't have her family together for Christmas, her heart was full of joy as she heard the children's gleeful laughter behind her.

She reached the front door of the shop as Jesper was walking out.

"Oh sorry, Frau Kindberg! I didn't see you there."

"We meet again, Jesper," Rachel laughed. "Merry Christmas!"

"To you as well!" He lifted his cap. "Sorry I can't stay and visit. I was sent to pick up the last of the carvings."

"It seems we're all rushing around after the snow." Rachel stepped to the side so Jesper could exit the doorway. "I'm excited for Elia to see the last pieces of her gift."

"They are quite exceptional," he said. "Not only is Elia enjoying each piece, but the entire castle is waiting to find out what the last pieces are and hear how the story ends."

Rachel laughed. "It has been quite the story. Please tell everyone at the castle 'Merry Christmas!' from Nils and me."

"I certainly will," said Jesper as he walked toward the castle.

Jesper

Jesper picked his way along the snowy walkways, careful to avoid icy spots as he returned to the castle. The frosty air burned his lungs but didn't dampen his spirits. It was Christmas morning, and although much daily work still needed to be done, Brigitta was preparing a fine meal for the staff.

He met several delivery people along the path, crying out holiday greetings. Waving, he held the two bags from the wood-carver close until he arrived at the castle and entered the kitchen door, where warmth hit him like a rolling tide. He knocked the snow off his boots in the entry and hung his coat on the hook by the door, the comforting smell of Brigitta's cooking filling his nose.

Vincent was at the table, having a cup of coffee.

"Ah, you're back, Jesper. Did you retrieve the last piece?"

"Actually, there are two last pieces. This one is to be given first." Jesper handed Vincent a blue bag. "The red bag is the last carving and the final part of the story."

Vincent's smile reached his eyes. "I see my friend has been very busy. I'm going to take these to the duke, who is waiting with Elia in her room."

"I thought she was feeling better," Jesper said as he warmed his hands by the fire.

"She is, but they are taking all precautions." Vincent turned to walk upstairs. "She'll play and rest in her room until the luncheon festivities begin."

Elia

Vincent tapped lightly on the door before entering Elia's room. Papa was reading to her as she sat on top of the covers, fully dressed. She was playing with the carvings spread out across her bedspread.

"I have the final carvings for you." Vincent handed Papa the two pieces and relayed opening instructions from the wood-carver before leaving the room.

"I can't wait to see what's next," Elia said.

"Two pieces? What a treasure Herr Kindberg has made you!" Papa offered the blue bag to Elia. "You open the carving, and I will read the story.

Elia's hands shook with excitement as she loosened the bag's strings and pulled out the woodcutter's cabin.

"It's the cabin in the woods!" she said, turning the carving around in all directions. "It will go right here in the middle of the rest of the carvings. I'm going to put Clara and Tucker McGinty beside the front door."

"Once you do that, I will read the next part of the story," said Papa.

Chapter 24

Pip

I waited until the couple left the barn before I took flight from my perch on a rafter. There wasn't much time. I had to see Grendela before the fishermen sailed, so I raced to the fishing village. I searched the woods, the barn, and the empty buildings before spotting her packed in a crate on the galleass, out on the water.

"Grendela," I called, landing on the railing of the ship. "I've come to report what's going on at the cabin."

"Pip, I'm so glad you made it before my departure." Grendela pushed aside two other geese. "Move over, you louts, I have business to attend to. Leena is not here, friend. So what's the news?"

"She gets to stay with the woodcutter and his wife," I reported. "And not just for the winter. Her uncle agreed to let her live with the woodsman and his wife forever."

Grendela honked loudly. "Forever! I can't believe it."

"It's true," I told her. "I heard the woodcutter tell his wife."

"That is the best news," Grendela said, great relief in her voice. "Now I can go back to Gävle knowing that the poor girl finally has a home. Thanks for letting me know, Pip. You're a good friend."

"Happy to do it," I said, preparing to take off. "I'll continue to watch the girl and what happens at the cabin. If you come this way again, I can give you a thorough report. Until then, safe travels, friend."

"Safe travels to you as well, dear Pip!" Grendela gave a joyful honk as I flew and the ship began to sail in a southerly direction.

Siv

I plodded along the trail without much trouble, my hooves sure. Thankfully, the snow had held off while Anders and I spent weeks of long days out in the forest. The days were tiresome, but Anders had some help from friends. The wood needed to fill his many orders, was all cut and stacked. When we returned home, Leena and Maja were waiting for us in the barn.

"Come, Siv. I have a bucket of grain for you." Maja took my lead. "You both have been working so hard, you deserve a treat."

I began to nibble on the tasty grain, then noticed Clara and Tucker walk into the barn with Leena.

"I brought you some cookies we made," Leena said, handing a small plate to Anders.

"A treat for me as well, I see." Anders chuckled as he winked at Maja.

Tucker walked to the pen where Lotti and Kola watched the goings-on, their heads stuck through the slats.

"There has been so much activity here; it's nice to see the three of them having time together," Lotti said to Tucker. "I wasn't sure our keepers would be able to work out having Leena stay. I'm sure glad they did."

"I tried to tell everyone that my master would work it out," said Tucker. "Anders is a fine leader, and with me by his side, we were destined to make it happen. Did I mention how my tracking abilities were vital in finding Leena in the fishing village?"

I grinned at Tucker's boasting, but Clara scoffed. "That dog has gnomes in the attic if he thinks he was the reason Leena came to live with us."

"He's a bit blustery," I told Clara as Leena brought me a bucket of water. "But he has a good heart."

"It sure is good to see Leena so happy," Clara said. "What a change from the bedraggled urchin that peeked over the bushes to ask for food."

"She is a sweet girl," I said between mouthfuls. "She brings me carrots and pieces of apple almost every day."

Anders finished cleaning my stall and was hanging up the pitchfork when Leena walked up to him. "I helped make cheese today," she said proudly.

"After she was through with her studies," Maja explained as she hung up my harness and lead. "We're going to have her caught up in no time so she can attend school after the holidays."

"Well, I hope you had some play time too," Anders said warmly.

"Oh yes!" Leena said. "Maja helped me make paper dolls. And we worked on a secret project."

"A secret project, you say?" Anders raised his eyebrows.

"It's for Christmas," Leena said, "so I can't tell you about it."

"Christmas is a long ways away," Anders teased as he rubbed down my coat.

"It is not," Leena protested. "It's in three days."

"Three? That can't be true." Anders shook his head. "It's a good thing we have all the wood orders filled. I have a secret project or two of my own I need to finish."

"Is one of your secret projects for me?" Leena asked, smiling up at him.

"Well, it sure could be, but if I tell you, it's not much of a secret." He laughed, tousling Leena's hair. Maja laughed too.

"Look at them. They all are so much happier. It's like they're a—" Clara cocked her head as if searching for the right word.

"A family," I mused, shaking my mane out of my eyes.

"Exactly," Clara agreed.

Leena

"It's Christmas day, Greta. You must be dressed in your finest for the holiday." Leena fastened a white apron on her docka.

Wonderful smells wafted into her bedroom, and her stomach growled. Leena giggled, reaching under the bed for a chest Anders had made for her from birch wood. She ran her fingers over the smaller limewood box stored inside. Retrieving her secret project from the chest, Leena placed it in her apron pocket and returned the chest to its place.

When she stepped out of her room, Maja and Anders were sitting next to each other, conversing in low tones. The table was adorned with a cheery red tablecloth and laden with porridge, saffron buns, and ham.

"Merry Christmas, Leena!" Anders said with a warm smile.

"Merry Christmas!" Leena said merrily.

"Come sit and have some breakfast before we open gifts. We don't have much time before we need to leave for church." Maja placed a cup of milk by Leena's plate.

"Could I give you your gift before we eat?" Leena asked shyly.

Anders nodded. "If you'd like."

Leena pulled out a scroll of paper, tied with a red ribbon, and handed it to Maja.

"It's for both of you," Leena said as she stood beside them.

"Thank you, my dear." Maja unrolled the paper to find a picture Leena had drawn of the three of them in front of the cabin. Written along the bottom of the drawing was the label "My family," and above the depictions of Anders and Maja were the words "Papa" and "Mama."

A silence fell over the room.

"Don't you like it?" Leena asked, biting at her lower lip.

"This is one of the best Christmas gifts I've ever received," Maja said, tears streaming down her face as she reached out and hugged Leena.

"Indeed," Anders said, bear-hugging them both. "We're so thankful you're part of our family."

Anders fished in his jacket pocket and brought out a small red bag tied with a green silk ribbon. "Leena, do you remember when I told you I would share my Father with you, if you wanted?"

"Yes," Leena said, leaning toward him. "You said you lost your family too but would share your new Father with me."

"Now is the time for me to do so, but first I have a gift for you." Anders handed her the red bag.

Chapter 25

Karl

With Elia's head resting on his shoulder, Karl read the line written at the end of the story that came with the carving of the cabin. "Please give the red bag to Elia." He felt a shiver of anticipation pass through his daughter's small frame.

Unlike the muslin bags the other carvings had come in, the red bag was made of velvet and was cinched closed with a thick green ribbon. Karl handed the bag to his daughter.

"Oh Papa, what's inside?" Elia asked, holding her breath. She gingerly untied the ribbon and handed him the scroll from the bag.

As she fished out the carving, he began to read the story. "Leena opened the bag. Peeking inside, she saw a wooden manger with a tiny baby peering up at her. 'I don't understand,' Leena said. 'What does a baby have to do with your new Father?'

"'Let me explain,' Anders said picking up a worn leather book. 'This Bible tells us of the Creator Father who made this world. This carving is of His only Son, Jesus, and it says in the Bible—For God so loved the world, that He gave His only begotten Son, that whosoever believeth in Him should not perish, but have everlasting life. Jesus was sent to earth to save us from the sin that had entered the world. The Father's Son grew up just like any other young boy to be a man. He shared the Father's love with all who would listen to Him. Ultimately, Jesus paid a dear price so we can one day be with our Father for eternity.'

"Leena stared at the carving. 'Even me?' she asked.

"'Especially you,' Anders assured her. 'God is the Father that gave Maja and me all of the ideas on how to help you. He promises to be the Father to the fatherless. You were and are never alone. God promises that He never leaves us or forsakes us.'

"'He is always working on our behalf, even when we don't see a way out,' Maja said.

"Tears began to stream down Leena's face, as a mixture of confusion, awe, and gratitude enveloped her. She was overwhelmed by the love and care the Father had shown her, a feeling she had never experienced before."

Karl felt a wave of love come over him as he cleared his throat and wiped tears from his eyes. He looked up and saw Elia holding the wooden manger to her chest, her own eyes moist.

The story and the carvings were not just toys to help Elia feel better, Karl thought, *but a message of love for all of us.*

"Is that all, Father?" Elia whispered.

"There's a bit more."

He cleared his throat again before reading on. "As Anders and Maja told Leena more about this kind Father, she became eager to share with others what she had discovered—that the Father's Son came to earth as the first Christmas gift, to show that no one is ever alone and that His love for us all knows no bounds."

"Oh Papa, what a wonderful gift we and the whole world have been given," Elia said as she cradled the manger. "I wasn't alone while I was sick. The Father was with me."

And with us, Karl thought.

"I can't wait to tell Mama how the story ends."

"Me either." Karl smiled and took Elia's hand. "Let's go find her."

Rachel

After Rachel and Nils returned home from church, she rearranged the items on the julbord table several times, wanting everything to be perfect. The julekake in the middle smelled of cardamom and was bursting with plump, juicy raisins. Several plates mounded with food filled the rest of the table.

Nils smiled when he finally came into their quarters from the shop. He'd had more customers after church this morning than he'd expected, each seeking a special gift.

"The shoppers have left to head home for their Christmas lunch," he said, sitting at the table. "This looks delicious, dear."

"We're almost ready," Rachel said, taking off her apron and filling the coffee cups on the table.

The bell over the door rang.

"Who could that be?" Nils said, getting up from his chair.

"I thought you closed for lunch," Rachel said, picking up a stray saffron bun that had fallen off the tray.

"I turned the sign to closed," Nils said, stepping back into the shop.

"Rachel," Nils called. "I'm going to need your help with this customer."

Rachel scurried to the shop, confused how she could help—until she stepped through the door and found Nils embracing Stefan. Their son gave her a broad smile over Nils's shoulder.

"Merry Christmas, Mama!" Stefan said. "Am I in time for Christmas lunch?"

Rachel couldn't believe her eyes. Their son was there with his ruddy-faced smile, his boots covered with snow and his bag dragging on the floor. Her heart swelled with joy at the sight of him, a mixture of relief and happiness washing over her.

"You're just in time, Stefan, just in time," she said, taking her turn at hugging him. "How did you get through all that snow?"

"I borrowed some snowshoes from a fella. I wasn't going to miss your cooking, Mama." Stefan placed his coat on his usual hook as the three of them passed from the shop into the family quarters.

"So your time away has not squelched your appetite at all," Rachel said, laughing. "Come sit at the table, and I'll get you a plate. We want to hear all about where you've been and what you've been doing."

"You had us worried, son," Nils said.

"Didn't you receive my letter?" Stefan asked.

"No. We had no idea where you had gone when you didn't return with the other young men. I wrote your captain and he told us he had postmarked a letter from you, but it never arrived. All we knew was what he told us—that you'd left with four other soldiers."

"I'm so sorry, Pa. I sent the letter so you would not to worry, Mama." Stefan stabbed a sausage with a fork and put it on his plate. "One of the guys in my barracks, Ulrik, received a letter from his mother. Due to unforeseen circumstances, her brother didn't have enough wood for the winter. Knowing Ulrik's conscription was done, she asked him to travel to his uncle's cabin to help restock his supply."

Stefan picked up a butter knife, slathered lingonberry jam on a saffron bun, and continued filling his plate. "Some of us fellas figured the restocking would go much faster if we all went. I wrote to you and then headed off with the group. When we arrived, we found out Ulrik's uncle not only needed wood for himself but supplied wood for several people in a nearby town. We got to work and filled all the orders, along with setting Ulrik's uncle up for the winter."

"That was a wonderful act of charity, son," Nils said. "I'm proud of you."

"I was able to grab a train in Gävle and planned on being home before Christmas, but the trains shut down when the snowstorm hit. I had made it to Kumla, so I borrowed a pair of snowshoes from a passenger living there and took off at daylight. The trek was only seventeen kilometers. We soldiers hiked farther than that on our military marches."

"I'm glad you arrived safe and sound," Rachel said, shaking her head as she enjoyed another sip of coffee.

Nils excused himself from the table and stepped into the shop. When he came back, he was carrying a large wrapped present.

"What's this?" Stefan asked.

"Your Christmas gift," Nils said, smiling.

Stefan ripped off the wrapping and stared wide-eyed at the large Dala horse Nils had painted blue with a yellow Nordic cross on each side. On the hindquarters, a union mark, combining the national flags of Norway and Sweden, reflected the union of the two countries since 1844.

"I wanted your gift to reflect how proud we are of what a fine man you've become," Nils said, patting Stefan on the shoulder.

"The carving is magnificent, Pa! Thank you so much." Stefan oohed and aahed as he continued to admire the horse.

"Hearing now about your recent adventure, we are even more proud," Nils said, adding more food to his own plate. "Was Ulrik's uncle sick? Is that why he couldn't fill his orders?"

"No," Stefan said. "He had cut all the wood he needed but given it all away."

"Given it away?" Rachel asked. "Why would he do that?"

"He was helping an orphan girl. She needed the wood." Stefan added more lutefisk to his plate.

Nils looked at Rachel, an astonished expression on his face.

"Oh, I nearly forgot." Stefan grabbed his bag from where he had dropped it on the floor. "Ulrick's aunt and the little girl that lives with them now sent me home with a gift as a thank-you." He pulled a linen sack from his bag and handed it to Rachel. She unwrapped the bundle and showed Nils a caramel-brown block.

"Gjetost!" Rachel exclaimed.

"It was true?" Nils whispered. He looked upward, raised his hands toward the ceiling. "It was all true!"

After looking at Nils quizzically, Stefan turned to Rachel. "It *is* gjetost cheese, but how did you know? I had never heard of it. Ulrick's family makes it to sell. It's very delicious and—"

Stefan paused to look back and forth between his stammering parents. "What's wrong? Do you not like gjetost cheese?"

Nils burst into a deep belly laugh, with Rachel joining in.

"What did I miss?" Stefan asked, his confusion adding to the humor of the situation.

"Well, Stefan, we have a story of our own to share," Nils told him.

Setting the cheese next to the julekake on the table, Rachel grasped her husband's hand and then her son's, giving the latter a firm squeeze. "Wait till you hear about the latest gift from the Creator."

Note from Author

This book began with a vivid image of a wood-carver. Each time I sat down at my desk to write, the wood-carver would come to mind, prompting me to find a picture, which I then added to a design board in my office. As the story unfolded, each new chapter brought a new character, adding more and more images to my board. Before I knew it, the board was brimming with both human characters and animal characters, a cozy cabin and a majestic castle, a galleass ship and a wood-carver's shop.

Initially, I had envisioned the setting to be in Germany, a country renowned for its vibrant holiday celebrations. However, the Father kept nudging me to research Sweden. I soon discovered the rich tapestry of Swedish customs, foods, and festivities, all steeped in a tradition of love and compassion towards others.

As I searched Swedish towns with a castle, I found Örebro and fell in love with the city. I watched videos, read travel blogs, and perused countless photos to add additional facts to the story. However, there is no "Kindberg's Woodcarving Shop" in Örebro but it would be fun if there were.

My local library brought in a treasure trove of research material on Swedish Christmas customs, life in 19th century Sweden, and wood-carving basics, which were vital for adding historical details to the book. After reading the woodcarving book, I watched hours of YouTube videos to learn the specifics of carving figurines, and I'm thinking of trying to carve a few figurines myself.

The character names came from online lists of Swedish names from the 1890s. When I came across the Dahl last name, I had to add it to one of my characters, as that was my great-grandmother Grace's maiden name. Duke Karl Vasa lived in the Örebro castle in the 16th century. Although all of his character details are fictionalized, I added his name due to the tremendous amount of remodeling and additions he made to the castle.

It was a joy to write this book, because it was a reminder to me and I hope a reminder to you of how extravagantly the Father loves us. As the characters found out in the book, He is always working on our behalf, no matter what obstacle or struggle we are facing. He is also there in times of creating, helping others, and joyful celebrations.

One of my favorite promises from His Word is "And the Lord, He it is that doth go before thee; He will be with thee, He will not fail thee, neither forsake thee: fear not, neither be dismayed."— Deuteronomy 31:8

Such comfort comes with that promise! May you rest in His love and peace, not only during the Christmas season but all year through.

Acknowledgements

—I want to thank my family for all of their support—
My dear husband, Dean—Becky & Coty, Lindsey & TJ, Megan, Christian & Caleb—Ariana, Addyson & Aubrey

My Mom, for years of prodding me to share my stories, and my siblings, for always supporting me in my newest venture.

Allen Arnold for "The Story of With" and sharing direction on how to "write with God." It has not only changed my writing journey but has strengthened my walk with my Heavenly Father.

Editor Jill Wilson, whose expertise and encouragement helped me overcome my hesitations and publish confidently.

Copyeditor and dear friend Janet Seegebarth, who has been cheering on my writing dream for years.

Beta Readers-Jessica Fouts, Kailee Sullivan, Pastor Jenna Schutt, and Janet Seegebarth

FlourishWriters leaders-Jenny Kochert and Mindy Kiker

The Battle Creek Library and librarians, Jessica, Mae, and Brandon for helping me with research materials for the book.

About the author

Marcie Sextro is a writer, creative, and encourager. With a love of Christmas and a passion for inspiring readers, she crafts vivid characters and the rich historical imagery that surrounds them. When she's not writing, you'll find her birding, gardening, or taking on her new creative venture in watercolor painting.

Marcie lives in Nebraska with her husband, Dean. Her love for her family is as deep as her love for writing. Marcie cherishes every moment she gets to spend with their five children, two sons-in-laws, and three beautiful granddaughters.

Visit her online at www.marciesextro.com.

www.ingramcontent.com/pod-product-compliance
Lightning Source LLC
Chambersburg PA
CBHW060755310726
48980CB00002B/108

9798993578705